D1106358

The Cat and the Jack of Spades

A Midnight Louie Las Vegas Adventure

Book 4

The Cat and the Jack of Spades

A Midnight Louie Las Vegas Adventure

Book 4

CAROLE NELSON DOUGLAS

Five Star
Unity, Maine

Five Star First Edition Mystery Series.
Published in 2000 in conjunction with Tekno Books
and Ed Gorman.

Set in 11 pt. Plantin by Minnie B. Raven.

Printed in the United States on permanent paper.

Library of Congress Cataloging-in-Publication Data

Douglas, Carole Nelson.
    The cat and the Jack of Spades / Carole Nelson Douglas.
        p.   cm.—(A Midnight Louie Las Vegas adventure ; bk 4)
    ISBN 0-7862-2896-2 (hc : alk. paper)
    1. Midnight Louie (Fictitious character)—Fiction.   2. Las
Vegas (Nev.)—Fiction.   3. Cats—Fiction.   I. Title.
PS3554.O8237 C22   2000
    813'.54—dc21   00-061050

For Mary Powers Smith,
an editor who's been a dream to work with,
thereby giving a publishing nightmare a happy ending

♠ Author's Foreword ♠

This is the fourth and last book of the Midnight Louie Quartet. These books were written in 1985–86, finally published two to a volume as *Crystal Days* and *Crystal Nights* in 1990, and until now have been out of print. They feature feline dude-about-Las-Vegas Midnight Louie, who acts as a self-appointed PI and part-time narrator in a current mystery series with twelve books in print: *Catnap, Pussyfoot, Cat on a Blue Monday, Cat in a Crimson Haze, Cat in a Diamond Dazzle, Cat with an Emerald Eye, Cat in a Flamingo Fedora, Cat in a Golden Garland, Cat in a Hyacinth Hunt, Cat in an Indigo Mood, Cat in a Jeweled Jumpsuit, Cat in a Kiwi Con.* The interior title alphabet that began with *Blue Monday* means there will ultimately be 27 books in the series.

The current Midnight Louie mystery series shares the same Las Vegas setting as the earlier books, but reflects the city's incredible building boom of the past 15 years (to which I have added fictional hotel-casinos, like the Crystal Phoenix and the Goliath that appear in the Quartet). Many of the secondary characters and backgrounds from the Quartet continue in the current series, forming a continuing universe. The Quartet is, in fact, the entire reason the Midnight Louie mystery series exists at all.

When the Quartet was sold to a category romance line in 1985, it was one of the first limited series within a romance line, and was the first to feature a feline PI narrator and include crime and mystery elements, anticipating trends that have become bestsellers since then. The romance editor enthusiastically bought the Quartet and received the first manuscript. Then something happened. The books were held from publication for four years, so long that the contract expired. During that time, I was promised various publishing dates and methods of publishing—the first book in hardcover, for instance—that never came about. A clue to the delay was in the editor's description of the books: "too mainstream, up-market, and sophisticated" for romance readers. Finally, the editor promised that the books would be well published and I would be pleased, and that they would be out within a year.

They came out in the summer of 1990, not in the romance line, but as main-list romances. And I was not pleased. Being removed from the line was not what displeased me, even though the books' low placement on the main list was essentially a "throwaway" spot. What got my (and Midnight Louie's) back up was that the editor had crammed the four books into two paperbacks containing two stories each. The 120,000-word length of the doubled-up books wasn't economical, so the editor cut each book up to 37 percent without my knowledge or participation. (I call this approach "cutting the body to fit the coffin.") I wouldn't have seen galley proofs had I not asked for them, and did all I could then to salvage the books within the ten percent of changes I was allowed before being charged typesetting fees. Even then the books did not meet my standards: plot elements seemed pulled out of the blue without preparation, mystery elements and deeper characterizations were stripped out, as were secondary characters. Forty percent of Midnight Louie's sections were cut.

I was convinced that the very elements the romance editor found "too up-market, mainstream, and sophisticated"—Midnight Louie's narration, the vivid Las Vegas setting, and the mystery/romance blend—were strengths, not weaknesses. Appalled by this unprofessional treatment from a major house, I "flipped" the concept and took Louie to the mystery side of the street, where he has been welcome indeed.

Midnight Louie, after all, is based on a real alley cat with awesome survival skills. He weighed eighteen pounds from eating a California motel's decorative goldfish, which had him headed for the animal Death Row until a cat-lover saved him by flying him to her home fifteen hundred miles away. Now the mystery series' publisher sponsors Midnight Louie Adopt-a-Cat book tours, at which shelter cats and kittens are brought into bookstores so we can find good homes for both books and cats.

In preparing the four novels for this, their first hardcover publication, I restored all the material that had been cut, including all of Louie's narrative sections. These were always briefer than they are in the current mystery series. Just having a cat narrator was daring enough in 1985–86. I made sure to keep his contributions short, if not sweet. Since the books were written as romances first, the mystery/crime elements are lighter than in the mystery series, but they involve a continuing puzzle that isn't solved until this, the last book.

Las Vegas has changed so much, so fast, and so radically since I researched the Quartet in 1985 that I've left the background "as was" to record what it used to be like. Because of the fast-forward nature of the Las Vegas scene, this is the pattern of the Midnight Louie mystery series too. The characters in the foreground move through a time period of months while the background buildings whiz by, reflecting years of construction and de-construction. It's like the early movies where the actors played a scene in an unmoving car while a montage of background scenes flew past. That's the only sensible way to deal with The City That Won't Stop Reinventing Itself.

So here comes Louie's last "original" Quartet novel again, in a new "authorized" edition. Previous novels in the Quartet have already been reprinted.

The credit for this successful revival goes, in the end, to readers, who live long, and don't forget. In that way, they're a lot like Midnight Louie, the alley cat who wouldn't die.

♠ Chapter One ♠

"She's back again."

Droning the words so softly that his lips hardly moved, the three-p.m.-to-eleven-p.m.-shift man leaned close to his replacement while he officiously tidied the barbell-shaped baccarat table.

The newly arrived graveyard-shift man's indifferent shrug permitted the chandeliers high above to polish the shoulder nap of his burgundy velvet evening jacket to a rich ruby glow.

Without comment, he straightened his formal black bow tie, eyeing himself in one of the mirrored strips that ringed the casino's baccarat area. No casino employee was more expected to embody discreet elegance more than a referee in the upscale Baccarat Cove where thousands of dollars might ride on one hand of cards.

The new referee's eyes finally flicked to a distant image in the mirrors that fenced him into his elegant cage.

He saw her immediately. Despite the constant hurly-burly of hundreds of people milling through the casino, he possessed an uncanny ability to isolate any individual instantly.

Also, she behaved with impeccable predictability. She always perched upon the stool marking the end of a long chrome row of nickel slot machines, just twenty feet from the semicircular risers that led to the exclusive baccarat area.

She was predictable in other ways as well. His eyes could never rest on her for more than scant seconds before she invariably glanced in his direction.

Once again, she performed on cue. He doubted she could be sure he was watching her from this distance; their tiny images ricocheted endlessly in the curved, mirrored wall. His eyes returned to his own image anyway—or rather, returned to the perfectly horizontal bow tie at his throat.

He never regarded himself face-to-face in mirrors if he could help it. This avoidance fed a sense of invisibility that he cultivated. He turned at last to answer the departing shift man.

"You're right." He smiled so tightly, it was almost undetectable. "She *is* back."

The three-to-eleven man shook his head. "I can't believe your cool, Solitaire. That lady's been camping out in that same spot every time you come on shift for four nights now. Don't it make you curious?" Grammar was not a prerequisite for baccarat referees.

"She's a tourist." Solitaire's distinctive low voice flavored his dismissal with a twist of Limey. "Tourists do strange things. And then they're gone. You've been in Vegas long enough to know that, Harry."

Harry shrugged and stuffed his Zippo lighter into the pocket of his own burgundy velvet evening jacket. It was a house uniform, but the only referee it seemed made for was Solitaire Smith. That's the way the man was. Everything seemed to come easy to him, yet he gave nothing back.

Harry paused at the top of the shallow stairs carpeted in burgundy plush to match the evening jackets. His fingers tapped speculatively on the chrome top rail.

"She don't seem too bad-looking from here, sport. So she's hooked on the nickel slots. Maybe she just wants a better view of you. She might be worth a roll."

"Not even dice are worth a roll," Solitaire Smith answered wearily. "Good night, Harry."

He turned to study the empty tables. Unlike craps, baccarat seldom attracted a crowd. Empty tables offered players a sense of exclusivity as they lost in a few minutes of gaming more money than Solitaire Smith made in a year.

Baccarat was the world's most understated way to gamble. Pure luck, not skill, determined the fall of the cards. The players dealt the cards; the winner held the bank. Solitaire's principal role was to approve credit and maintain order. It was perhaps the key position on the casino floor.

A well-tended man in formal wear slowly mounted the stairs and sat at a table. He would be joined shortly by others of his ilk as quietly—oh, so quietly—they began to lose the sums that kept hotels like the Crystal Phoenix and cities like Las Vegas, Nevada, and tight-lipped baccarat referees like Solitaire Smith solvent.

Nowhere in that ordered scheme of things was there room for a mouse-haired tourist with a fondness for nickel slot machines, late hours, and watching a stranger in a burgundy velvet evening jacket across a crowded casino.

"Golly, Gayle, are you *still* here? I thought we came to Las Vegas to have fun! Oh, let me sit down, my feet are killing me!"

"That's what wearing spike heels while walking the Strip all night will do," Gayle answered sensibly. She sipped the free drink the cocktail waitress had delivered an hour before and slipped another nickel into the slot.

"What's so fascinating about this particular machine anyway?"

"It's my lucky spot," Gayle answered with a rueful smile. She paused before pulling the lever to study her friend.

"Don't fuss over me, Kelly. I'm having a fine time."

"A fine, dull time. Gayle, the whole idea of bringing you to Las Vegas was to have some fun, maybe even meet some men."

"Is that where Connie is?"

"Yeah, she met this neat English stockbroker at the Dunes. I scrammed since I was definitely a third wheel in the process of rapidly going fat." Kelly absently fanned herself with the souvenir program from the Lido de Paris floorshow, blowing back the precisely rolled curls of her hot-combed Lady Clairol blonde hair. "Maybe you're just too refined for Las Vegas."

Gayle raised an unplucked light brown eyebrow. "Maybe. But I'm having fun right here. Honest! I've won . . . eighteen dollars in nickels."

"And you'll lose it all again by morning. You always do. That's not why Connie and I talked you into this trip, hon, to sit by yourself and shake hands all night with a slot machine."

"I'm not by myself."

Kelly studied Gayle's serene profile. It was delicately etched against the darkly winking casino ambiance, like a reversed silhouette, emphasizing the creamy white skin that she considered her friend's only outstanding feature.

Otherwise, Gayle had predictably brown eyebrows, brown eyelashes and brown hair that she wouldn't bleach, frost, tint, highlight or spray with punk pink on Friday night just for fun.

Gayle had brown eyes, too, that you couldn't really do anything dramatic with, which was why two savvy bachelor girls like Connie and Kelly had taken her under their collective wings all the way from Canton, Kansas, to wicked, with-it Las Vegas. Twelve million gamblers couldn't be wrong.

14

"We just thought," Kelly said slowly, speaking for her absent soul sister, "that it's been eighteen months since . . . Joe . . . and that you needed, oh, to get out and about a bit."

"I'm here! I'm fine. I'm happy. Don't let me cramp your style. I won't get back to the room until after breakfast if you want to bring somebody in—"

"Gayle! I'm not that kind of woman—well, not usually anyway. Here I'm trying to tell you what's good for you, and you want to throw me into the arms of the first man whose eye I can catch."

"People who keep telling other people what's good for them generally get pointed in another direction."

Gayle pulled the handle again, listening to the machine grind through its motions until cherries, a lemon, and a pineapple lined up across the playing window. A pittance of nickels clattered into the chrome coin bay at the bottom.

"Cherries up in the first row. I win something!"

"Peanuts," Kelly diagnosed in disgust. She pushed herself back up on her magenta snakeskin Liz Claiborne heels. "I'm going out looking for some fun," she announced. "I guess I'll know where to find you."

"Sure," Gayle said serenely, plunking another nickel in, in the nick-el-o-de-on.

Alone again, Gayle glanced toward the Baccarat Cove. Three tables were occupied now. At one, an elderly male player partnered a thirtyish blond wearing a long, strapless beaded gown who looked as if she'd just stepped out from a Lincoln Continental ad.

Gayle couldn't see her quarry at the moment, then found him: at the woman's side, bending to retrieve the glittering evening bag that had slid from her silken lap to the carpet.

He straightened smoothly, as he always moved, deliberate as a bullfighter. The woman leaned forward, décolletage spilling over the caviar beads trimming her strapless bodice rim, to reclaim her bag.

He deposited the shining purse on the table, turning to supervise play once again.

Gayle exhaled her burning, hoarded breath, then rammed five nickels, the maximum allowed, down the slot machine's cold chrome throat.

At a quarter to one in the morning, Solitaire Smith pulled back the gilt French-provincial chair for the cool blonde with the hot neckline.

Her sugar daddy was leaving, so her only recourse was to lean lushly into her impressive décolletage as she rose and toss Solitaire a warm parting glance as gamblers throw tips to the table.

Some casino employees played the mating game with guests. He didn't. Besides, an unlikely sound had distracted his alert ears. The small squalling of an infant.

He went immediately to the curved barrier separating the privileged baccarat area from ordinary casino action. A petite woman in a fringed buckskin jacket and blue jeans leaned against the chrome and Plexiglass railing.

"You're missing the finale of Johnny's second show," Solitaire noted.

"I know. But you-know-who wouldn't sleep, so I've been walking here and there." The woman tossed her head twice, shifting wings of long dark hair over her shoulders, and reached to unfasten the knapsack on her back. "I thought you might like a peek at the frog princess."

Solitaire's smile became a trifle more discernible. "I hear she's got her father's voice."

"Tell me about it." The woman rolled expressive hazel

eyes. "A born Streisand. Or a yodeler. We're not sure which." She peeled back the inner yellow blanket to reveal a small, sleep-puckered face.

"What are you calling her, Jill?"

"Samantha Jane," the mother grinned, automatically swaying in a slight, constant rock. "Or brat, depending on her behavior. I don't suppose you want to chuck her under the chin or something," she teased.

"Heaven," he answered firmly, "forbid."

Jill grinned. "Poor Solitaire. Always so predictable." She turned away from the rail to face the casino itself, then stopped rocking for a moment. Samantha Jane protested. "She's there again."

"So I've been told," he answered dryly.

"I figure she's got a crush on you."

"Her hard luck."

"She looks like a nice lady."

"Nice ladies don't get crushes on me."

"Oh, I don't know. Listen, how about a little advice from a mother?" He snorted at her bland self-description. "Do something different for a change. Be nice to her."

"Being nice is against my principles."

"You've been nice to me and Johnny, and if you hadn't told Steven about the sheik's son, Darcy might be doing the hula in some harem instead of the chorus-line kick at the Crystal Phoenix."

"Those were accidental oversights," he told her. "Now get that underage brat out of the casino or I'll sic the owners on you."

"Sure," she sneered good-naturedly. "I'd like to see Van and Nicky take on Samantha Jane in a shouting match. 'Night now."

Whisking the blanket over the infant's head, Jill hefted

the baby on her back again and made her way through the madding crowds, unconcerned.

Solitaire shook his head with an expression that passed for fondness on his stoic features. On anyone else's, it would have been called noncommittal.

He checked his watch, an expensive Swiss timepiece that put him on temporary semi-equal ground with his monied players. He liked and needed that small eighteen-karat edge. If he weren't refereeing baccarat, he would have worn any Timex that ran—and, in his long and circuitous past, had usually done just that.

Just one a.m. and six hours to go, he noted automatically. Some days the nights seemed extra long.

He glanced at the last slot machine on the third row across the way. She was looking his way, all right. They stood as close yet apart as they had ever been. She blinked, twice, but didn't move. For a moment he held her gaze, then turned back into his plushly carpeted, almost-empty domain.

The players arrived and departed in slow, stately turns, like transatlantic liners gliding into port. Invariably male, often dressed in evening clothes, they came in a polyglot of models—English, French, Austrian, Spanish. They were all as rich as Onassis and most were about as personally appealing. Sometimes they amused him, sometimes they bored him, but he never envied them.

Seven o'clock finally stole into the casino's frenzied twenty-four-hour cycle. Solitaire gratefully ceded his turf to the morning man and moved thoughtfully down the wine-colored steps, his eyes on the mirrored black-patent-leather toes of his shoes.

At the bottom, he paused to look up.

She had swiveled on her stool to face him, her ankles laced around its legs, an oversize paper cup of nickels braced on her lap. She looked like a kid at a soda fountain. She looked pleasant and ordinary and quite, quite sane.

Her lips parted, either to speak or simply to allow her to breathe more deeply. Solitaire Smith spun on the smooth soles of his evening shoes that had never trod anything but carpeting. He quickly left the casino floor through a door marked Employees Only.

"I guess Kelly took my advice."

"*Hmmmf?*" Connie shook her tousled ash-brown mop free of the sheets. "You back already, Gayle? I just got in a few minutes ago, it seems like."

"It's eight-thirty in the morning." Gayle kicked off her shoes and moved into the bathroom. "The last time I saw Kelly, she was heading back on the Strip. How was your stockbroker?"

Connie groaned and held her head. "I can't remember, but all he talked about was making money, so he must have been interesting. What did you do all night? Keep that slot-machine stool warm again?"

"Yeah," Gayle's voice outsang the running tap water.

"Oh, heck, Gayle. We just thought you'd have a good time here, that's all. God knows you deserve a good time. And we're going back to Canton Tuesday morning. Back to the bank jobs and the snow. I mean, it's March here, for heaven's sake, and it's warm and they have no snow! And the place is crawling with eligible men and—"

"—and gamblers and hookers and loudmouths and drunks." Gayle came out of the bathroom foaming at the mouth, her paste-whitened toothbrush in hand.

"And baccarat referees." Connie, more awake now, smiled slyly.

Gayle froze. "So you figured that out."

"It's not hard. Something besides winning and losing nickels all night's gotta be keeping you at your appointed post. Listen, it's great if you're attracted to some guy— that's what we're all here for! Only that man wouldn't give you the time of day in the shade of Big Ben!"

"He doesn't . . . overreact," Gayle admitted wryly.

"And you're the last woman he'd react to. Those rich broads come and go under his nose all night. It'd take more than sitting thirty feet away for a few nights to light his fire, and you're not about to do anything more."

Gayle sat at the foot of Connie's bed, atop the navy spread imprinted with beige phoenix medallions.

"Maybe you're right."

"Sure I'm right. Give it up. Come out nights and have some kicks with us. I guarantee you'll have more fun than mooning after some guy you've got an insane crush on."

Gayle nodded soberly. "You make a lot of sense. Except I haven't got a crush on him." Her perfectly ordinary brown eyes focused with extraordinary sincerity on Connie's sleep-dazed gray ones. "I love him."

Connie's mouth dropped unflatteringly open and stayed that way.

♠ ♠ ♠

"Wouldn't you know that our mysterious Mr. Smith, late of places and faces unknown, would attract an equally mysterious admirer? What is this—the fifth night in a row?"

Van von Rhine cocked a taffy-pale eyebrow in the direction of the end slot machine, then turned amused marine-blue eyes on Solitaire Smith.

"Does *everybody* know about that?" he demanded.

"Face it, Smith," said Nicky Fontana, Van's husband. "A

guy who hardly puts zip on his employment application can expect to attract curiosity, especially if some moonstruck doll suddenly parks her crinoline on his doorstep when he's never been known to tumble for anything in skirts."

"She's a perfect stranger," Solitaire began.

"Perfect," Van interjected, looking significantly at Nicky. "He likes her already."

"—and something of a pest, besides being a damn fool. I don't know why she'd want to make an idiot of me, but she's making a worse fool of herself."

"Why is she making a fool of herself because she likes to look at you?" Van inquired. "It seems a relatively harmless pursuit."

"It's not," Solitaire snapped. "I don't like being the talk of the hotel. For God's sake, I didn't do anything to attract her attention. I wish she'd go back to Kankakee or whatever dismal town claims her and leave me alone!"

"My, my, and her a paying customer, too." Nicky donned a mock frown dark enough to match his Mediterranean coloring as his voice took on the playful tone his Uncle Mario used on occasion. His Uncle Mario, a leading Las Vegas entrepreneur, had occasion to use more than a tone of voice, including hired muscle and firearms. "The nickel slots haven't had such a faithful follower since the Leopard Lady was last in."

"It's not funny," Solitaire said. "I don't want the bloody woman."

"I know," Van murmured. "*You vant to be alone.* All alone. Forever alone . . ."

His eyes blazed challenge. "Yes. That's right."

"We're leaving," Nicky said in pacification. "It's nearly one o'clock and I gotta get the old lady to bed." Van bristled. "Me, I think being alone stinks, but then I come from a large family."

Solitaire's hands tightened around the chrome top rail between them.

"Take it easy, Smith," Nicky counseled with more compassion. "Women get notions and forget notions just as fast. Besides, this is Monday. If she came in on Thursday, she'll be leaving tomorrow. None of 'em stay much over the weekend. They can't afford to."

"That's right," Solitaire repeated slowly. "She'll have to leave soon."

Van leaned nearer to tap the top of his white-knuckled hand. "And then you'll be all alone. Again. I guess you're just lucky."

♠ ♠ ♠

Her friends had given up on her. Gayle wasn't sorry. She hadn't felt like talking to friends, explaining herself again. She wanted only to talk to the man across the crowded casino, but she didn't know how to.

"Oh, I'm a fool," she told the impassive face of her slot machine, feeding it another nickel.

The man clearly resented her presence; likely other people had noticed that by now, too. Maybe they'd send a security guard to eject her, charge her with loitering with intent to drool . . . Gayle grinned and sent another nickel to noisy oblivion.

Connie had lent Gayle her peach charmeuse disco dress with the padded, sequined shoulders and petal skirt to match the frivolous, peach-satin heels Gayle had bought for her sister's wedding. Kelly had extended makeup application and perfume. Tonight, Gayle looked about as enticing as a respectable woman from Canton, Kansas, could get and still sleep soundly.

Yet an unbridgeable distance yawned between her and

the nameless man in the burgundy evening jacket. A long way. And the three women were booked back to Kansas on the ten-twenty a.m. flight tomorrow from McCarran Airport.

Gayle selected three fresh nickels and looked up. He was watching her coldly, the man she had told Connie she loved, watching her as if he hated her and maybe hated her even more for looking so nice tonight.

The nickels clinked in sequence down the long metal tunnel. The man was still returning her long-distance look, and she couldn't glance away if her life had depended on it.

What was his name? What did he like to eat, read, play? Why had he commanded her attention from the first night, when the three women had settled for a drink in the lobby lounge and Gayle had suddenly seen him in the baccarat area?

Her thoughts clattered together like nickels, striking unmelodiously as they turned, echoing, swelling into a chorus of clinks, thundering like hail or applause or your own heartbeat when you're paying too much attention to it.

Somebody was pulling on the sleek sleeve of Connie's dress.

"Honey. Honey, you better start catching those coins in something, or they're gonna bruise your insteps when they fall. Honey, you won! You got more nickels pouring into your lap than Santa Claus has Christmas presents."

Gayle wrenched her eyes from the man so far away to study the woman milking the slot machine beside her. Nickels poured with unholy haste from her own slot machine's bottom. They chuckled sharply into the chrome payoff tray. They bounced and piled and overflowed and slid off her lap to the navy carpeting—nickels as populous as fleas, shiny silver nickels worth nothing separately but now propagating shamelessly.

Glancing up, Gayle saw a trio of golden bells in the machine's window. She reached for empty coin cups and began shoveling nickels into one, then a second, third, fourth, and fifth. People had gathered around to *ooh* and *ah*. They blocked her view of the man across the way, and she was glad he couldn't see her anymore—sitting on her stool like an enchanted peach toad on its lily pad—while nickels erupted all around her.

She was hopeless, Gayle thought as money poured out from her lucky pull of the lever. Tomorrow the man would be just a memory, a haunting soft-focus image to burn into the clouds outside her plane window on the flight home.

By the time the onlookers dispersed and her nickels made impromptu weights of a dozen giant-size paper containers, Gayle still inhabited an unhappy daze. She risked a peek at the baccarat area. He was gone. A stranger in plain evening black had taken his place.

Las Vegas casinos were kept dim night and day to encourage gamblers to mislay time and common sense. At the man's absence, the shimmering canopy of light above Gayle seemed to ebb as if at a touch to a distant rheostat. He had vanished on her last night here—it was almost morning, actually—and that probably was a sign.

Gayle carted her paper cups to the cashier's marble and chrome cage, friendly strangers offering her a hand. She watched a computerized change machine swallow her homely nickels, add up a liquid crystal total, and return $842 to her.

"Fifties or twenties?" the cashier inquired cheerily.

"Uh, fifties. I guess." She had never carried a fifty-dollar bill before, although she'd handed out plenty at the bank. Even in that high denomination, the payoff wad threatened to choke her doll-size evening purse.

Still trying to force the tiny gold prongs shut, Gayle edged away from the cashier cage to let another winner or loser transmute money into other forms.

She'd won. Elation swelled in her, then met an odd sense of loss and trickled away. Head down, eyes on her suddenly valuable purse, Gayle walked into something. A man.

"Say, aren't you the little gal who just made the slot machine over there say uncle?"

"Yes."

"You're a lucky one! Come on, girlie. Give the dice a salute for luck before I throw."

People gathered around watched him pull her toward a nearby crap table.

"Oh, I don't know anything about this—"

"You don't have to know anything. Just give the dice a blow from those sweet strawberry wine lips of yours, honey. I'll do all the work. I'll throw 'em and make 'em sing. Blow, honey, blow!"

Startled and dazed at the same time, Gayle watched the man's fist shaking almost angrily before her face. Inside it, dice clicked like rattlers. Outside it, heavy gold rings shaped into horseshoes and oil derricks flashed a broad be-diamonded wink.

She blew at the dice on his open palm as if they were candles on her birthday cake, too soft and too hard at the same time.

Then the dice were tumbling across the navy Ultrasuede—every other casino in Las Vegas used the traditional green felt, but the Crystal Phoenix prided itself on being different, Gayle remembered reading in its brochure.

The man beside her was yelling and crooning, shouting strange phrases and numbers.

"Aha!" His sweaty hand squeezed her waist. "You're my little lucky charm, sweetie. Come on, kiss 'em again. Blow, baby."

They all watched her, all the fevered faces packed around the table. Only the two men in the navy house vests seemed calm and sober. A waitress dipped behind her, dispersing drinks. Gayle clasped one before she realized what had happened. The man beside her had half drained his already.

"Blow!"

She did, feeling puzzled and silly.

The dice tumbled away and then stopped.

"I don't know what's hotter, the dice or my little gal's lips," the man was crowing. "Give me those bones. What's your name, sweetie?"

"Gayle."

"Gayle's gonna bail me out and onto easy street. Blow 'em home, baby."

"I've got to go—"

"Go? You can't go." His hammy hand, hot with gambling fever even through her dress, corralled her. "Nobody leaves a crap table when the dice are hot. And you're making 'em go, go, go! Come on, now, one more time."

There was one more time after that, and another. Perspiration beaded Gayle's forehead and gathered unseen between her breasts and shoulder blades. Everyone around the table cheered as the dice hopped this way and that, and landed right every time. She sipped her drink for coolness, grateful when a passing waitress pulled the almost empty glass from her hand to replace it with one still full of unmelted ice.

"Bah-*low!* Am I lucky? Have I got an eye for winners, or what?"

Then the dice cooled. They rolled to a stop, and everyone stared and suddenly quieted. The man's custodial grip on Gayle's elbow tightened. He rattled the dice before her face again, imploring her to blow.

Feeling as winded as Moby Dick, Gayle sent an exasperated breath across the small cubes. The man cast them away from him like diamonds he wanted to watch shine as they rolled. They landed as they always did, with a different configuration of spots. For reasons Gayle couldn't understand, the fall was bad, and the man's money was rapidly thrust down a slot in the tabletop to oblivion.

"Better quit, man," voices were murmuring. "They've iced."

Feverishly, his eyes studied the dice, the tabletop with its cryptic designs, Gayle's face. "Okay," he said. "Okay." He backed away from the table rim. "I'm quitting while I'm ahead. I mean it. I'm walking away now." His expression brightened. "And I'm going to take my little lucky charm and celebrate!"

"No! I've got other things to do." Gayle tried to wriggle loose from his grasp, but his huge hand closed possessively. "Please!"

"Come on, baby, you helped me win a pot! Now I'll take you out and spend some of it on you."

"I didn't do anything. I don't know anything about this game. Let go!"

He was pulling her down the crowded aisle, her high heels snagging in the thick carpeting. In a moment, he was at the cashier's cage where his pocketed piles of chips came back in high piles of fifty-dollar bills.

"Come on." He had never released her elbow and now stuffed the bills into his pockets with one hand. His florid face was indistinguishable from the faces of a hundred middle-aged gambling men around her. "We can start with a drink in my room—"

"No!" Gayle shouted. Men were outshouting her at crap tables all up and down the casino. "No! Let me go!"

He was dragging her with him. In the chaos, their progress looked normal for Las Vegas, just another happy winner hustling a bimbo back to his room for a quick between-game lay . . .

Gayle elevated her foot and smashed the needle-sharp heel onto his instep. He was wearing boots, and the blow glanced off impregnable leather.

"Hey," he roared, turning on her.

"Hey," came a low voice nearby, "why don't you take your winnings and stick it . . . in the hotel safe. Mate."

Gayle felt the man's hand on her arm loosen, then clench, then loosen again. His face hardened, then winced as it stared into the eyes of whoever stood behind her. The gambler backed away, edgy and resentful.

"I guess you went cold on me too, baby. Here, Gayle—a cut for your trouble."

He pulled a wad of bills from his suit-coat pocket and thrust them down the front of Gayle's borrowed dress. Fire erupted in her cheeks, but the man had already spun on his cowboy-booted heel and was gone.

Gayle turned to her rescuer.

He was tall, although not imposingly tall, a couple inches under six feet. She lifted grateful eyes to his face. And, like the man who had just left her, froze as if seeing a Medusa.

There was no visible reason to freeze; the man's features were harmonious under a frame of dark chestnut hair. The deliberately dim casino lighting concealed such details as eye color, but his mouth remained taut with unuttered threat and his eyes were guarded. Grimness grasped them as a bezel holds a jewel, but even now was relaxing its grip. Slightly.

The man's hand had commandeered her other elbow, as if claiming equal time in manhandling her. Then Gayle realized he merely thought she might fall over.

She nearly did. He was so close she had almost not recognized him—the baccarat referee she had been watching for five nights straight.

"I understand," he said politely, "that you've been looking for me, in a manner of speaking."

♠ Chapter Two ♠

"Hadn't you better retrieve the wages of your sin?" the baccarat referee asked.

"Wh-what?"

In answer, his first and second fingers slipped behind the surplice bodice of Gayle's dress and plucked the folded fifty-dollar bills free. Not so much as the edge of his fingernail brushed her, but the bill edges had produced a slow parting tickle across her skin.

Before she knew which to do, blush or burn, he had drawn her toward the cashier's cage.

"Evening, Blanche. Some fresh fifties for the young lady. These . . . fell into bad company."

The cashier swapped the sweat-limp bills for crisp new editions as cheerily as she conducted all her transactions.

"There you go, Solitaire, new bills for old."

Solitaire. Gayle flashed a startled look at his impassive face. He presented only his profile at the moment, an intent, neatly etched jigsaw puzzle piece that fit the slow, measuring survey of her eyes.

His lips moved silently, and then he turned to Gayle. "Two hundred fifty. Our gambler was generous in his rage— or too ham-handed to be tight-fisted with his money." He thrust the five bills toward Gayle.

She backed away, into the polished marble column of the cashier's cage. "I don't want it."

"Of course you do. I've already 'laundered' it."

She eyed it askance. "Still, I don't need it, really!" She shuddered a little in remembrance of the gambler's unstoppable energy and restless, tension-slick hands.

"Everybody needs money," the man called Solitaire said so flatly that she looked up quickly to make sure his lips had moved, that he had spoken at all.

"I already won tonight—plenty."

He said nothing but impatiently thrust the money toward her.

Gayle reached for it. "If you would share it with me, as a token of my thanks—"

His fastidious fingers released it so quickly that she barely caught the bills before they fluttered to the carpet.

"I don't happen to be one of the everybody who needs money. Or thanks." He turned to go, the folds of his burgundy velvet jacket light-burnished to the color of rose-gold.

"Wait." Her palm rested on his forearm. The velveteen cloth reminded her of the plump, wine-velvet-upholstered Victorian settee in her grandmother's house in Canton that she'd loved to wriggle into on rainy days as a child. "Please . . . Solitaire."

She couldn't tell which offended him most, her touch or calling him by the same name the cashier had used so casually.

"Let me at least buy you breakfast!" she offered in glib desperation.

"I don't eat breakfast," he said brusquely, turning back into the crowd, turning away into the distance that grew darker with every step.

"I do," Gayle said a little too loudly, her throat tightening on a sodden lump of disappointment.

He glanced over his departing shoulder, paused, then turned back. The crisp cuff of his evening shirt retracted under his fingers to reveal a glittering gold watch face.

31

"Two hours, then. After I'm off. I'll pick you up at your home address."

She parted her lips to ask where he meant, but his wry grimace anticipated her.

"The slot machine two stars to the left and straight on till morning, remember? Seven a.m., right?"

"Seven." She nodded. "I hear it's a lucky number."

"I don't believe in luck."

"Just like you don't believe in breakfast?" She tried to sound bantering. He took her dead seriously.

"Just like I don't believe in a lot of things you probably take for granted, like the sun rising in the east every morning and wishing on a star every night."

He left so smoothly that she didn't know she'd been abandoned until the crowd milled around her without the comforting buffer of his presence.

Gayle shook herself alert again and glanced toward her Las Vegas "address." An interloper occupied the stool in question—her stool. Someone who'd seen her win had slipped into her spot in the mistaken notion that a slot machine that pays off once will do it again, and soon.

Gayle headed for the rest rooms, ignoring the interior bubbling of a heady half-and-half brew, composed equally of hot triumph and cold feet. In the long noncommittal mirror, she freshened her makeup and patted her forehead with a damp paper towel.

She perched on a taffeta-upholstered boudoir stool, feeling like Miss Muffet about to encounter a most intriguing spider face-to-face in due time, and refolded all her hard-won bills into as tight a wad as so much money could make.

Her own less gilded watch face revealed that it was five a.m. and she had almost two hours to kill. She did it by leaning her chin on her bracing palm, letting her focus blur and replaying the brief minutes with Solitaire into an endless mental chain of sight and sound and speculation.

Two hours later, Gayle was installed on her customary stool, her bill-laden purse clasped protectively upon her lap, her feet neatly paired on the lowest rung.

The baccarat area lay deserted except for two referees, neither of them Solitaire. It was seven-fifteen, and he hadn't shown. She licked dry lips, visions of regaling her roommates with a report on her breakfast fading. She could approach the other referees to ask after him, but the railed-off baccarat area seemed as set apart from the ordinary gaming congregation as a church sanctuary.

Was he having, she wondered, a good laugh about it? How funny to convince the naive tourist that he'd be there and then to leave her waiting and wondering! No, he wouldn't—or rather, she didn't think he would from what she knew of him, which was nothing . . . and everything.

Gayle ran icy fingers up her silky-sleeved arms, momentarily unguarded. The purse on her lap tilted and slipped to the floor.

"Oh, darn."

She leaned forward to retrieve it and found herself looking down on a head of polished chestnut hair. Green eyes flashed up at her in sudden proximity, then lowered to the neckline of her dress.

Gayle straightened, pressing the gapping crossover flap shut again, feeling the silver heart-shaped locket she wore fall back against her breastbone.

"Thank you," she said as he stood and handed her the bag.

"My pleasure," he said as cryptically as always, but the words cut two delicious ways. Maybe he'd intended them to.

He knew what she wanted and he knew she worried about it.

"I was looking for the velvet jacket," she explained quickly.

"Costuming," he answered, contempt seasoning his tone. Self-contempt. "Las Vegas is the world's greatest sideshow. Where'd you like to go on your last morning?"

"How did you know?" She stood slowly, trying to adjust to a hero in blue jeans, plaid shirt, and navy windbreaker. Out of formal dress, his face looked deeply tanned, almost weathered, an odd effect on a man who thrived in a late-night, hothouse environment.

"Tourists always leave on Tuesday."

"Oh. Guess we're . . . *I'm* fairly predictable, then."

"Yes." He softened slightly. "And no. I'd rather not eat here if that's all right. We can move down the Strip. All the hotels have coffee shops. Or did you have something pricey in mind, now that you're flush?"

"No, just . . . breakfast. I have to get back by nine at the latest. The plane—"

"When's your flight?" he asked, leaning on the tinted-glass exit door to hold it ajar for her.

"Ten-twenty."

"Cutting it rather close, aren't you?"

"Yes." She raised bold eyes to his face.

His expression froze for a moment, then tautened into amusement. It could as easily have hardened into menace. "Quite the gambler, aren't you? I should have a name, I suppose."

"Gayle." He said nothing. "I don't like it much either, but that's what they put on my birth certificate, and I'm stuck."

"I've heard worse." His hands were in his pockets, and

his eyes squinted into the morning sunlight streaming across the desert flats and straight into the low-profile streets of Las Vegas like the Cannonball Express. "Anything more to it?"

"Tyson. I'm from Kansas. And you?"

"Smith," he said shortly. The caged amusement that so often danced across his sharp features cut loose for a step or two. "I'm from . . . everywhere."

"Why do they call you Solitaire?"

"Because it's true."

"You must have a real name."

"Don't you like 'Solitaire'?"

She paused to think a minute. Milling people mindlessly parted to flow around them. "It's . . . costume," she said, a mirroring twist of dismissal in her voice.

His hard green eyes squinted down at her through the deep auburn thicket of his lashes. Their color reminded her of ferns and black cats, of oriental jade and wet early morning grass.

"Nicely done, Kansas," he conceded. "You catch on fast."

His hand closed on the back of her arm. "Here, let's try the Dunes. We haven't much time before you leave."

The booth was upholstered in orange vinyl, the tabletop formed of brown walnut Formica. Hanging ferns tickled the tops of their heads. They had managed a window table, only because Solitaire had spotted it the moment they entered the coffee shop and had piloted her toward it so purposefully that no one dared race them for it.

"Why the observation post?" he asked abruptly as soon as the waitress had taken their orders and their coffee cups were full.

"You mean . . . in the casino?"

"There are others?"

She did blush this time and bent her head to blend half-and-half into her coffee. "No, just there."

"Why? Why waste your time in the entertainment capital of North America warming a slot-machine stool?"

"I don't know much about gambling. Playing that seemed safe."

"Not if you were making eyes at me."

" 'Making eyes'? Who was making eyes? I've never made eyes in my life!"

"Ah. You do have some pride."

She started to protest even more, then paused. He was right; she'd made a fool of herself for days, nights, on end. In public.

As if released by her confusion, Solitaire Smith leaned back against the garish orange vinyl. "Look at me," he said. "I might as well get a decent inventory of my not-so-secret admirer before she goes. After all, you've been feasting your eyes on me for long enough." Irony interlaced his words.

"Not in broad daylight," she flared, aware that he had leaned into the window-side corner of his bench, so the light fanned past his unreadable silhouette to whitewash her face.

"I just know how to play my cards better," he murmured. There was more of a smile in his voice than she'd heard before, now that his features were dimmed. She blinked past him into the bright light outside and said nothing.

He took his time, partly because he could be cruel in his own defense, partly because his curiosity had been piqued. He'd managed to keep a great many far more sophisticated people at an icy distance, why was this rather undemanding woman so unshakable?

She submitted to his rude, silent scrutiny with resignation, sipping her steaming coffee, gazing past him to what she *could* see—the verdant hotel courtyard outside with its oblong turquoise pool.

Solitaire studied her as he would a painting. Bright morning sunlight brushed cinnamon highlights into the honeyed swirls of her relentlessly ordinary medium-brown hair. Her eyes echoed that harmony, their brown a warm mélange of milk chocolate and caramel. Her face was softly shaped, with no one feature dominating, and her mouth had a fresh fullness that seemed untouched.

But it was her skin that was extraordinary. Fair, fair as an alabaster rose in an English garden, easily burnished skin that would burst into ripe red bloom on her cheeks and lips when conditions—wind, shame, passion—called for it. Creamy satin-smooth skin that rebuffed sunlight and made carefully cultivated tans seem boorish. Skin a man who nightly wore a velvet jacket, whose fingertips slid over Ultrasuede playing surfaces and slick pasteboard cards still might find himself unsatisfied with his life if he did not touch it once.

Solitaire felt the mask of taut muscles he wore slip. He let it sag another notch. He studied her hands—gardenia-pale, too—but economical in movement as she lifted the cup, circled the spoon.

Earlier, he had rather cynically perused the artless drape of her neckline, the subtle cleavage so pathetically uneventful compared to the expert unveiling achieved by the worldly mistress who'd paraded her charms to the lowly hotel employee last night—a taunt to both the wealthy man who had to buy her body and the poor man she'd lend it to for nothing, despising them both.

The woman he studied now despised nobody. A sterling silver heart at the swell of her breastbone caught his eye—a sweet, unassuming, Kansas kind of trinket. It must mean something, he thought. She wouldn't do anything unless it meant something to her. And then he realized what that insight meant to him and sank deeper into the corner seat, into his own self-generated shadow.

The waitress swooped over the table, depositing thick restaurant ware heavy with the pale foods that passed for breakfast in American coffee shops everywhere.

Gayle glanced down at her breakfast. Scrambled eggs and pale toast festooned with an orange curl and tiny parsley parasol.

"Are you done?" she asked calmly, picking up her fork. "I wouldn't want to deprive you of equal time."

"I have the feeling," he answered, pushing himself out of the shadow, his daily mask in place, "that you wouldn't want to deprive me of anything."

Her fork paused in midair. "I thought you didn't have any feelings."

"Ah. First pride, then pique. Next, you'll be hating me."

She thought about it, her camellia cheeks turning peony pink. "No," she said, looking steadily into his eyes. "I don't think so. There are some ways I'm *not* predictable."

The nylon windbreaker screeched across the vinyl like chalk on a blackboard as he shifted rapidly into position before his breakfast, a more colorful Mexican omelet that Gayle wished she'd ordered.

"So what's not predictable?" he asked. "Where you work?"

"A bank?" Gayle smiled to think of the bank in Canton with all its smug, small-town brick security. "Hardly. It's horribly predictable to work in a bank."

His head tilted quizzically. "Not really. Most women who work in banks are weighed down with enough gold rings and chains to deck an Arab bride. And they wear long, painted false fingernails. Or did you leave yours at home?"

Now her head tilted. "You're right! I'd never thought of that. I guess it's because female tellers handle so much money and make so little of it. They need to wear their wealth, not unlike an Arab bride. But I'm not a teller, I'm"—she pinked modestly—"assistant manager. How did you know about tellers?"

"Elementary, my dear Gayle. They all end up in Vegas, flashing their golden goodies as if they were rich girls. Most women who work in banks are drawn to money—or men who have it."

Still warmed by the sound of her name in that carelessly intimate phrase, Gayle cooled as his last implication took ugly root in her pride.

"I'm not," she said sharply. "Drawn to money, that is. I work in a bank because the president was a friend of my uncle's, and in a town as small as Canton that helps you get a foot in the door after high school."

"No college?"

"No college. In a town like Canton, girls are still supposed to get married and have children."

"Did you?"

She chewed her scrambled eggs far longer than called for, then inhaled deeply before answering. "Yes. And no."

For a man who disdained breakfast, Solitaire Smith had made fast work of his omelet. He pushed away the plate and the topic of conversation at the same time.

"I've gotten too personal, haven't I? Sorry. It's against my religion. I owe you penance. Ask me something."

"Really?" Brown eyes glinted dubiously.

"Really." Green eyes narrowed. "I can always take the fifth amendment, as you Yanks say."

"As we say . . . you're not from this country, are you? Where are you from?"

"You don't buy 'everywhere'?"

"I work in a bank; I've seen counterfeit bills before. Besides, I love the way you say 'elementary' and 'rather'—you're from England, or were originally, right?"

He lifted his hand to scratch ritually at the bridge of his nose. The first gesture she'd seen him make effectively obscured his expression.

"Would you buy Australia?"

Gayle sat back cogitating, schoolgirl style, hands primly clasped on the table rim, eyes cast toward the ceiling. She mused, one of her more effective expressions.

"Look at me," she ordered finally and half playfully, as he had commanded her minutes before. Solitaire sent her a look that exploded from the undergrowth of his eyebrows like a mine. It made her want to blink and apologize for taking liberties, that look, but she could submit to it just long enough to read truth in it—among other, less direct and more devastating things.

"Australia it is," she concluded.

"Now you know it, forget it."

"Why?"

"*I* have."

"Didn't you like it there?"

"Like it?" He seemed truly lost for words. "Are you finished?" he asked abruptly. "You've got to get out of the hotel in half an hour to make your plane."

"My plane . . ." She'd forgotten about it, about Kelly and Connie and the bank and Canton, Kansas. Completely.

He was reaching into his back pocket for money and she started belatedly. "I said I'd get it."

"Just the tip." Two dollar-bills floated to mid-table.

Gayle's eyes widened. One would have done.

"Relax, Miss Tyson. You're not playing bank manager here. Hotel workers in Vegas get minimum wage. They live on tips."

"Like you do?"

His smile came like a state secret, for her eyes only. "I am paid respectably for my rather invisible talents. And I get tips, too, handsome tips."

"Did *she* tip you?" Gayle wondered.

"She?"

"The slinky number with the constantly slipping purse and strapless dress. Last night."

"Oh. She." He was no longer smiling as he trailed Gayle to the cash register. He leaned on the counter and searched among the after-meal mints as if they were exotic fruits while Gayle waited for her change. "In a manner of speaking."

Solitaire kept his eyes down, remembering finding the hundred-dollar bill in the side pocket of his evening jacket.

"She" knew she would be back again tonight or next week or next month or next year, afflicted with her calculated brand of dropsy, and wanted to be remembered until then. Women who had everything always wanted something they couldn't have and were adept at spotting it.

Gayle didn't try to pry apart his silence. They quickly wove their way through streaming people to the street. Outside, he pressed a silver circle the size of a half-dollar into her palm.

41

"A tip for madame."

Stunned, Gayle stared at the humble foil-wrapped mint in her hand. "I didn't notice you buying it."

"The hand is quicker than the eye, particularly in Vegas."

"Thank you," she said belatedly. "I've never had my palm crossed with silver before."

"Think nothing of it," he advised her, his serious, ungiving gaze underlining every word.

"You don't . . . give people things much, do you?"

Instead of answering, he twisted his wrist so that the rich watch sparkled against the homely navy sleeve of his jacket. "I give them warning when they're about to miss their planes."

He took her arm and hurried her along the sidewalk and into a side door of the Crystal Phoenix.

"I guess I *am* late," Gayle fussed, her high-heeled feet stuttering alongside his Western boots as they hurried through a long, dim service hall. "Oh, I wish—"

He stopped her with a savage jerk. "Don't wish. There's no percentage in it."

Inside the hotel, his eyes and mouth had grown grim and guarded again. Gayle felt a bit afraid of him. His fingers, tight on her upper arm, loosened fastidiously, as if they'd forgotten themselves. "Say hello to Kansas," he said softly. "The elevators are through that door."

She turned to glance where he had pointed. By the time she turned back, he was melting into the distance and the dimness, just a silhouette in a long hall, walking away.

"Solitaire—"

He didn't turn.

"Good-bye," she said, too late to be heard by anyone but herself.

"Gayle Tyson, where on earth have you been?"

Gayle paused on the threshold to the hotel room, seeing chaos in the process of becoming more chaotic. Clothes were flung in every direction, dresser drawers sagged open, suitcases gaped untidily.

"The airport limo leaves in ten minutes! What on earth kept you?"

She wanted to tell them. She wanted to sit them down on one of the disordered beds, grab their wrists, and whisper hysterically like a teenager.

"Guess what, you guys? I had a *date* with *him!* Well, not a date, exactly, but we had breakfast together. We saw the sun rise practically. He even bought me a (poignant sigh) mint. He has the most beautiful green eyes and I think he kinda likes me and oh, I like him, I do, and he wants me out of town fast, he likes me so much—isn't that wonderful?"

But it hadn't been like that, except for the out-of-town part. It hadn't been like anything Gayle had hoped for.

Tonight would come so fast, and Solitaire would be there in his "costume," in his handsome burgundy velvet coat and handsome cast-iron face. Everything would be the same in the Crystal Phoenix casino, as it had always been. Except. She wouldn't be there. She'd be home in Kansas, in her quiet apartment again, in her office at the bank under the overhead fluorescent lights that sometimes flickered blue.

But they didn't flicker like neon, no. Not like neon. Maybe if she came back to Las Vegas, next year, he'd still be there in the baccarat area. Maybe, but Gayle wouldn't want to see it, to see Solitaire as another handsome fixture installed to console the tourists while they lost their money.

"Why are you hanging onto that evening bag, Gayle? Let

go. Kelly's dug out your regular purse. Gayle!"

"Money," she croaked. "I won some money."

They wrested the evening bag away, Connie quickly unzipping the back of Gayle's dress.

"Whew! Lots of money!" Kelly reported as the tiny purse sprang open on its wad of greenbacks. "I'll jam it in your big purse. No time to put it in the billfold. *Umh!* All *fifties.*

"I'm so glad you got *something* out of this trip, hon! Connie, hand me the purse and I'll pack it. Gayle, get moving! We left your black suit out for traveling. Hop into it. You'll just have to wear the shoes. I don't know where I stuck your wedgies."

Between them, Kelly and Connie dispatched Gayle's belongings into her half-packed bags, dressed her, and double-checked the corners of the room for left-behind items.

Gayle stood dazed amid their urgency, knowing that it swirled around her, and rightfully, but unable to feel it. What she did feel was like a kid who'd taken a nasty spill on a sidewalk, who suddenly knew that the world could fly up and make her knees bleed when it wasn't supposed to be that kind of place.

Standing there, Gayle didn't know how to help them, or herself, or even the man called Solitaire. Frozen by her own confusion, she wanted only to stand and bawl at the surprise and pain of it all.

"Look at what this staying up all night has done to you, Gayle," Connie clucked in a motherly tone, grabbing her elbow and hustling her out of the room. "You look beat! I'll bet you'll be glad to get back home to Kansas. Kelly, have you got the room keys? I forgot. Oh, good. I can't wait to get on that plane."

"Speak for yourself," Kelly said as she waddled down the

hall under the burden of a wardrobe bag and an overloaded carry-on. "*I* can't wait to get on that plane and find out how Gayle won all that money! I guess the nickel slots paid off after all, right, Gayle? What a little fox!"

The Araby Motel clung to the Las Vegas outskirts like a wart. It was brown, low, and sprawling. At night, the missing letters in its neon sign blinked intermittently black in gap-toothed splendor. By day it more legibly advertised Waterbeds, Cable TV, and Air-conditioning.

The last announcement told the tale of the Araby Motel. Quality motels and their guests took air-conditioning for granted.

Solitaire Smith took nothing for granted but one simple fact he seldom liked to think about. He pushed it out of his mind now, walking home to the Araby Motel.

Instead, he thought about Gayle Tyson clicking her peachy pink high heels together and leaving Oz on the Mojave for Aunty Em and Kansas and maybe even a small black dog called "Toto."

He didn't have an Aunty Em or a dog or even a home, and hadn't in twelve years—or maybe never. And he walked the long, dusty blocks between the Crystal Phoenix and the Araby Motel because he didn't have a car.

Cars came with license plates that could be traced and sat in open parking lots, inviting notice. A man could walk a different route to the Araby Motel every afternoon and morning if he were careful and fade into the shadows between the sunlight and the neon.

He had the money to stay in a nicer place than the Araby Motel. The Crystal Phoenix job paid well enough. But nicer places came with neighbors who clocked comings and goings, who noticed the names and faces of tenants. And the one thing that Solitaire Smith could not afford was to be noticed.

Crushed pizza cartons and rolling beer cans littered the Araby Motel's empty parking spots. Solitaire stepped over the refuse, precise-footed as a cat.

His room was dim, the curtains drawn as always over the single unbelievably dirty picture window. This morning it looked drabber than usual. Even the lurid velvet paintings of Elvis Presley and a bullfighter above the two single beds refused to brighten its dullness.

He ripped off his jacket and threw himself down on one of the cheap floral bedspreads without bothering to remove his boots. Later, he would sleep.

Now he listened. He lay still as death. Finally, a distant drone from not-too-far McCarran Airport made him lift his head to consult his expensive wristwatch.

Ten-twenty-five. Right on time. Up, up, and away in a silver bullet, wafting out of Oz and back to Kansas, with three clicks of her pretty peach satin slippers. The way out of an ugly Oz. The milk run to Kansas.

He wished for a moment that he had an atlas so that he could check what city her flight would land in, speculate whether she would change planes somewhere, and wonder when she'd get home.

But he didn't have an atlas. He owned nothing he didn't need. This tawdry room was too small to house anything more. Sometimes he moved too fast to take even essentials. At times like those, he didn't need silent witnesses to leave behind—a book, a photograph, a memento of a past he always shed like dead skin.

Gayle Tyson's past, present, and future came in a tidy predictable ball, like well-saved string. He wondered how long exactly it would take her to forget him, to return to apple-pie normalcy.

And she would go home, to normalcy and forgetfulness. Stories always ended that way. Only one thing bothered him in this one, this happy ending that reached all the way to Kansas.

He wondered most of all how the Tin Woodman, if he didn't have a heart, knew enough to want one.

♠ Chapter Three ♠

Midnight Louie Reflects on Character

Some think that solitaire is about the only game of cards that is not played in Las Vegas.

This is a fatal error; for Las Vegas, if it offers the world anything, presents ample opportunity for assorted individuals to go their own assorted ways. Nobody much cares as long as doing so does not fracture a law too old to bend gracefully.

The night-shift pit boss at the Crystal Phoenix does not drink, smoke, gamble, or play tiddly winks, for example, but this does not impede him from earning his daily bread in the drink-hazed, smoke-fogged betting environment of a major casino.

Solitaire Smith is like that pit boss. He lives in Las Vegas and works in Las Vegas, but he is not *of* Las Vegas, if you are able to hitch a ride upon my drift. He is my kind of dude, to tell you the truth. He does his best work at night, minds his own business, walks softly, and keeps his lips buttoned tighter than the shrink wrap on an issue of *Penthouse* magazine.

Like myself, he gets around, but he does not advertise this fact, so I am more than somewhat surprised to see him skulking over to the Dunes one morning. Everyone with any sense in Vegas knows that when the sun comes up, Solitaire Smith vanishes until Dame Nature pulls the fluffy white curtains closed on the west window of her quaint little living room each night and the sun goes down as quiet as a German silencer.

Then I see that alongside Solitaire's elderly gray-lizard boots is trotting a set of feet attired in shoes of an entirely different persuasion—being skimpy, high-heeled, covered in peach satin and decorated with rhinestone bows on the toes.

Why, you could bowl me over with an ostrich plume.

Solitaire Smith is known to be the quiet type, and nowhere is he more quiet than around the ladies. You must understand that I am not able to get more of a lowdown on the reason for Solitaire's sudden desertion of male solidarity, since I see the world from the sidewalk's-eye view.

But I hot-paw it back to the Crystal Phoenix, resolving to tuck myself into the deepest, darkest, softest corner I can find to mull over this startling change in habit. Nothing interests me more than the vagaries of human nature. So I am barreling through the lobby in my usual efficient but understated manner, when I receive my second shock of the day.

Face-to-face with me—and I do mean face-to-face, eye-to-eye, nose-to-nose, lip-to-lip, and whisker-to-whisker—is an extremely sophisticated female personage attired from head to tail in the finest white chinchilla coat I ever saw—walking at least.

This fur is not only white, it sparkles silver on the tips. The lady's feet, too, are artistically presented, each small curved nail being painted platinum by some practitioner of the grooming art at an upscale emporium.

The enchanting creature's wide-set, piquantly angled sea-green eyes (I never saw the sea in my life, but I know what is what anyway) are edged in jet-black, like the mascara the big dolls wear, only this looks like the genuine article.

This natural platinum blonde addresses me in a low, throaty murmur and proceeds to brush past me, stranding several long white chinchilla hairs on the sleek black sides of my best business suit. (It is also my only business suit, but what the hell.)

Naturally, I am not so rude as to point out the drawbacks to her unprecedented familiarity, especially to a small doll whose neck is wrapped in what looks to be a twenty-four-karat-gold choker with an extension as long as the little lady herself, which extension sways upward like a swami's rope.

The only thing missing is a snake, and I apprehend that the prime candidate for that role is a tall doll likewise attired in full-length fur of a non-naturally acquired variety at the leash's other end. She is talking to my bosses, Mr. Nicky Fontana and Miss Van von Rhine, and she is full of things to be unhappy about in advance.

It somewhat piques me that Mr. Nicky Fontana and Miss Van von Rhine (she is really Mrs. Nicky Fontana in private life) fail to acknowledge my presencet—here are times when undercover work is taken for granted—but then they act more than somewhat flummoxed by the tall doll and her complaints. Finally Miss Van von Rhine takes matters into her own dainty little hands, and says like this:

"Please, Miss Ashleigh, desist in engaging in noises of a hysterical nature in the lobby. I am certain that you will find your suite satisfactory and more than somewhat cushy for the tastes of your obviously refined and discriminating feline companion. Please allow us to attend to installing you in your quarters and we will worry about suitable entertainment for Yvette as the need arises."

Two things impress themselves on my razor-edged intelligence: Miss Ashleigh must be Savannah Ashleigh, the film star. And Yvette—well, the little doll before me bats snow-white eyelashes as the two tender syllables of her name echo high above us.

We know ourselves to be alone in a world of plodding passersby—passing by Hush Puppies, Famolares, Tomy Lamas and Adidas . . . I hear music, and there is no one there—it is too early for the lounge pianist to be scratching the keys as if they were a kitty litter box or for Chef Sing Song to be whistling en route to his carp pool.

Yvette. How can I express all that is contained in two, short, thoroughly classy French syllables like that? *Yvette*. I forget Solitaire Smith. Let him attend to his own tawdry affairs. Midnight Louie is embarked on the *tendresse* of the decade. *Toujours l'amour*. Louie l'amour. *Toujours* class. I have found my Waterloo and *c'est moi*. Don't fire until you see the greens of their eyes and all that stuff.

Now where was I? Oh. Solitaire and the peachy-footed doll. Solitaire who?

♠ Chapter Four ♠

"Solitaire broods all alone in his lair,
    Safe at long last from young ladies who stare."
The baccarat referee in the burgundy velvet evening jacket turned from the empty tables he tended. The squat, indifferently attired figure of Nostradamus, bookie-about-town, posed dramatically at the top of the royal ruby stairs.

"*E tu,* Egbert?" Solitaire asked sardonically. But his glance automatically darted to the end slot-machine the third row over. It looked unusually deserted this evening. "You're not the first to point that out to me tonight."

The rhyming bookie shrugged, ignoring the reference to his true given name, a fact he held as close to his literal vest—a checked model in particularly loathsome shades of green—as a hot tip on a horse race. He thought for a moment, then his seamed face tightened diabolically.

"I suppose you're pleased now, friend Sylvester,
    That the lady who looks is no longer a guest here."
Solitaire grimaced. "*Touché,* as they say in the swash-bucklers. I'll forget your real moniker if you'll forget mine. We must break into the same personnel files."

"Done." Nostradamus grinned and glanced again toward the unoccupied stool. "Gone?"

"Yes," Solitaire breathed ardently. "What's the matter, mate, haven't you got enough odds to occupy you that you have to scrounge the local gossip? She was a five-day wonder, that's all. Balmy little bird from Kansas."

"Kansas, she says, is the name of the star."

Solitaire waited for the next line, glaring.

"A line from a song I heard in a bar," the bookie finally explained.

"Ruddy unlikely. It's from *The Wizard of Oz*."

"My . . ." Nostradamus leaned on the spectacular railing with its columns of clear Plexiglas supporting a sinuous length of polished chrome.

"You do get around for a foreigner.

But don't count on her any more in here."

"Thank God! And haven't you got anything better to do? I escape one kibitzer and acquire another. I shan't miss being the centerpiece of her attention, believe me."

Nostradamus's arthritis-curled fingers touched the bill of his plaid cap. With one last rhymed set of monosyllables, he left. "A lie. Good-bye."

"Liar yourself," Solitaire growled good-naturedly at the bookie's slightly crooked vanishing back. He turned his attention again to the empty gaming tables littering the Baccarat Cove.

Moving from table to table, he began searching for lint on the rich burgundy Ultrasuede fabric. He aligned the rows of chips in their grooved slots at the table's narrow necks and checked the decks in the plastic "shoe" that dispensed cards much less larcenously than a human dealer might have.

Everything was spotless and correct. Each end of the barbell-shaped baccarat tables mirrored its opposite side, rounding out to a well-padded Ultrasuede rim, the numbers one-to-seven and eight-to-fifteen dividing the playing areas.

Solitaire liked taking his seat at the notch in the table neck and watching wealthy men amuse themselves into states of less wealth. He relished presiding over such an ordered, rule-governed environment, predictable in every respect but the fall of the cards. He liked observing, aloof yet invisibly in control, while everyone forgot his presence. That appealed to a man who dared not be predictable, who could not afford the luxury of being noticed.

"A penny for your thoughts."

He turned to confront the latest rail-bird. A tall limber woman had twined long, blue-jeaned legs around the rail; her face—in full stage makeup—tilted inquisitively in his direction.

"Sorry, madam. The lowest wager here is five hundred."

"A bit beyond my budget." She grimaced, then glanced around. "I came to scout She-Who-Watches-and-Waits, but she must be gone already."

"I'm afraid so, Darcy Dancer."

"You mean you're pleased as punch! You haven't any romance in your soul, Solitaire."

His expression never changed. "You mean I haven't any soul."

Darcy regarded him for a moment through the thick shadows of her long false eyelashes. "Sometimes I wonder . . . Well, you can't blame me for being curious."

"Aren't you due back on stage to shake some feathers, or something, rather soon?"

" 'Or something' is more like it." Her impudent nose wrinkled. "It's the between-show break. I can come up and mingle if I want to."

Throwing a leg over the top rail as if it were a ballet bar, she arched her body sideways until her fingertips touched her pointed foot. She grinned gamin-style at Solitaire sideways. "I bet you found some female attention flattering, anyway."

"No, I didn't," he answered crisply. "I was annoyed."

"Oh. I get the hint." Her hyper-extended leg swept to the floor. "But I wish I'd eyeballed the woman who could set her heart on such an unrewarding target."

"No doubt a masochist who enjoyed the rejection," he answered icily.

"No one enjoys being rejected," Darcy retorted. "Not even—I'd bet five-hundred dollars—you." With a farewell smile, she was springing with the dancer's endless energy through the leadenly milling casino crowds.

"Is my business so endlessly fascinating that everyone has to poke his or her nose into it?" Solitaire asked the air under his breath.

The air declined to answer him. They all, he knew, would have liked him to fall to the single-minded tourist from Kansas. He had proven too impervious to the blandishments that Las Vegas exists to offer—gambling, drink, women. When one is wholly self-sufficient, he mused, others yearn to see that self unsettled.

He glanced to the slot machine in question, then froze to see a figure perched on the stool, pumping nickels.

It was only Hester Polyester—one of the local landmarks—an elderly lady with white hair rinsed iris purple, an inexhaustible wardrobe of pastel-shaded polyester pantsuits and a command of foul language that would have made Nostradamus blush.

She caught him staring at her. Solitaire winked. Hester Polyester's screwed her sallow-grape face into a prune of distaste and kept nickels chiming down the long stainless steel esophagus leading to the machine's insatiable stomach.

The first baccarat players strolled up the plush stairs. Solitaire donned his official face, which differed little from his unofficial face, and went to greet them.

At midnight, exactly, Solitaire looked up from a hot game of baccarat, uneasy about a sudden charged shift in the atmosphere. He felt watched. The slot machine stool stood askew and empty.

He surveyed the casino, focusing on faces with lens-like efficiency. None rang warning bells in his almost photographic memory. But new hounds could have picked up his trail by now, he thought. It made no sense for the same ones who had failed in Sidney and Bangkok to be here.

Perhaps he liked this job too much, had stayed too long, had become too much of a fixture in his froggy-come-a-courtin' velvet coat and by now too-noticeable effacement. Perhaps, he thought, glancing idly over the scene he had grown accustomed to, it was time to . . .

His eyes, automatic screening devices that they were, had skimmed the slot machine rows again. Now they froze. He rose abruptly, nodding to the other referee to spell him at the table. The players frowned at this breach of etiquette during a game, but Solitaire was already striding down the burgundy-carpeted risers toward the slot machine.

"What in hell?" he demanded when he got there.

Gayle looked up from the machine, an undispatched nickel clutched between her thumb and forefinger.

"Was that 'hell-o'?"

"That was supposed to be good-bye. Stand up."

She remained seated. "Why? Are you going to hit me?"

"I don't hit women—yet," he amended between gritted teeth. "What in bloody hell?"

Solitaire glanced around to see slot machine enthusiasts poised with nickels clenched between their fingers, their eyes and ears fixed on him and Gayle. He sighed, then extended an open palm like a headwaiter indicating a table. "Come on."

"Are we going any place interesting?"

"The Crystal Promenade. I need a drink."

She preceded him mutely down crowded aisles thick with clatter and bodies, across the casino aisles, to the meandering string of lobby cocktail lounges that circled the Crystal Phoenix's main floor.

Gayle felt a firm hand close on her upper arm. The white terrazzo at her feet seemed to heave deliriously. Shafts of deliciously giddy excitement darted down her arms.

"Here," Solitaire was saying tersely, steering her efficiently toward a tiny marble-topped table paired with two peacock-backed white wicker chairs. A florist's jungle of parlor palms dripped like weeping willow around them.

Nearby, an artificial stream meandered, its tinkle echoing the keys on the mirrored grand piano where a white-armed woman in an evening gown was playing rippling chords.

"This is nice," Gayle began, charmed by the discreetly choreographed atmosphere.

"It's a place to sit and talk in privacy." Solitaire's attempted cordial nod at the arriving cocktail waitress more resembled a glare.

Gayle mentally reviewed her limited repertoire of cocktails. None appealed tonight, but then she was extremely tired. After all, two long airplane flights in one day could be exhausting. "A . . . tequila sunrise," she finally decided. They were quite the thing in Canton, Kansas.

"Cuba libre," Solitaire said curtly.

Gayle's sleep-defrauded eyes widened. "I hate to ask if that's a drink—or a secret password."

"Rum and Coke with a dash of lime," he explained, resting an elbow on the table and pinching the bridge of his nose, his eyes shutting momentarily.

"I thought you didn't drink."

"I don't—often." His eyes suddenly blinked open, boring

into hers. "All right. What are you doing back here?"

"It's a free country."

"No. No, it isn't."

"I suppose you're an expert."

"I am, as a matter of fact. Oh, it's freer than most, but no place is free. You're avoiding the question. Why—how in hell—did you get back here?"

"By plane," Gayle answered meekly. "Late flight. I wanted to simply turn around, once I got to Canton, but there were things I had to take care of."

"I thought you had to get back to a bank job."

"That's one of the things I had to do. I quit my job."

Profanities stumbled on the threshold of his mouth, fading into inaudible lip movements. Gayle watched him adoringly. "You quit? My God, woman, how will you live? You must be mad!"

"I've got some . . . insurance money. For a while. I've never done what I wanted in my life, always what other people thought was sensible, so I thought I'd try it—once. And I didn't want to leave Las Vegas."

"You're back at the hotel?"

"Yes."

"And back watching me."

With her shoulders straightened and eyebrows lifted challengingly, Gayle suddenly looked less fatigued. "Yes."

"But why?"

"I didn't want to leave yet."

"Why?"

She wished her drink were here; she could have used some tequila courage. "You."

The flat of his hand slapped the marble, releasing a violence that made Gayle blanch. She bit her lip and waited.

Solitaire's eyes, which had roamed their surroundings as

if seeking an exit through the parlor-palm jungle, returned to hers. Their expression was not encouraging.

"Gayle, you can't camp out on my figurative doorstep night after night. Oh, I suppose no one will kick you out—if I don't ask them to, and I could, you know. Casinos have total discretion as to whom they let play in their precincts. A nod from me, and you'd be rather rudely escorted out the door by the security guards. You have no idea what kind of a world you're playing so fast and loose with."

The waitress came, enforcing silence, and placed Gayle's long-stemmed glass on a gold-phoenix-emblazoned black napkin. Solitaire's drink looked like no more than a tall glass of Coke.

"So why wouldn't you have me kicked out?" she asked after sipping through the straw embedded in her rosy-hued drink.

"It's not cricket. You really haven't violated any house rules. And"—he sighed again—"I don't want to humiliate you. Although you seem to have no qualms about doing the same to me."

"I'm not trying to embarrass you."

Solitaire bleakly studied Gayle. Her soft features had curled into a look of troubled concern. Her brown eyes hovered big and sincere over the soda-fountain shape of her drink. If she'd been a worldly woman, he could have handled her better. More brutally.

"What are you trying to do?" he asked quietly.

"I don't know. What I have to, I guess. It's hard to explain, most of all to you. I just . . . *saw* you. The first night we came. That was all. I seemed to know you—"

"No one knows me." The dim lighting kept Gayle from seeing the color of his eyes, but she knew that if green could burn, they would be a raging forest fire by now.

"They respect you," she argued. "I can tell. Your friends—"

"What friends? I don't have any friends!"

"Sure you do. Those people who keep stopping by. Everybody around here has to touch base with you. Don't you see it? You're this very stable . . . magnet on the casino floor, everybody's drawn to you—"

"You're raving mad! I hardly talk to anybody, except in the course of my job."

"What about the short wizened man tonight?"

"A bookie!"

"And the tall girl with the dancer's legs?"

"A fellow employee. I know her only in passing."

Gayle smiled. "You know a lot of people in passing, Solitaire. And they like you. I'm not the only one. You don't see it, do you?"

"No. You're fantasizing again. I keep to myself because I like it that way. And no one knows me, not really."

"I know. I know you like it that way. But, I can't help it! I know I . . . do. Know you, that is. And I"—her polished pearl-pink fingernails bent back the corners of the black cocktail napkin—I want you," she added in a low voice, looking down.

In the ensuing silence, the lounge pianist began the lush runs that introduced a new song. Her soft, husky contralto, throbbing with vibrato, sang the single, opening word.

Des-per-ah-do . . .

Gayle sighed deeply, her eyes still watching her fingers fold and unfold the napkin corners. When Solitaire spoke, the timbre of his low voice vibrated in unconscious unison with the woman's singing.

"I could be married," he warned.

She looked up. "Are you?"

"Gay," he threw at her next.

Gayle rolled her eyes. "I may be from Kansas, but *please!*"

"A criminal. A child molester."

She laughed. "Those things would be easy for you to be compared to what you are. I think you're . . . well, whatever it is, it isn't that easy, that black-and-white. What *is* your sexual preference, anyway?"

"Celibacy," he snapped.

This time she believed him. "You could do it, couldn't you? Even in Las Vegas."

"Especially in Las Vegas," he answered. "You've got a nerve, to show up here and watch me for a few nights and say you know me, want me. I don't know you. I don't want you." Each word came out clipped and definite. "That should settle it."

She shrugged and sipped mournfully on the tequila sunrise. "It won't go away," she complained.

"What 'won't go away'?"

"The . . . feelings. They're really rather awful. Listen to me! 'Rah-ther awful.' I'm starting to talk like you. Maybe I'm just terribly suggestive."

A smile quirked unwanted at the corner of his lips. He controlled it. "Suggest*ible,* I believe you mean. Go on, what feelings?"

"It's rather personal."

"If you can sit there in front of the entire casino and make me look like a bloody idiot, you can certainly confess your girlish yearnings to the object of your desire. Come on, chin up, ducky. Men have to do it all the time."

Her head rose, some of the sunset concoction in her glass bleeding into her cheeks. "They do, don't they? And that isn't fair. All right. Here it is, chapter and verse." She folded her hands and took a deep breath.

Solitaire lounged resignedly into the shadow of his high-backed chair. "I have a feeling I'm going to regret this."

"I just saw you, and I couldn't stop looking at you. Everything else went sort of out of focus. And then you noticed me, and every time our eyes met, I got these, these flu symptoms. Maybe it was more like being on a roller coaster at the county fair, though I haven't been on one since I was thirteen, or a falling elevator. I couldn't think about anybody or anything else, I had these fireworks exploding inside me like it was the Fourth of July, I was going hot and shivery by turns. I was a mess, but—"

"I can hardly wait."

"But I liked it. No, I *loved* it. Then I started thinking crazy things."

"That's something new?"

"I started wondering what the color of your eyes were, how tall you were—not because I care but because I want to know how we would . . . fit together. I tried to figure out how I could get closer to find out all these things. I wondered if I'd like your voice, if you'd still make those sparklers go off inside me."

"*I* don't do that to you, Gayle. *You* do it to yourself. You and this wild fixation of yours. If it hadn't have been me, it would have been someone else."

"I've seen dozens of 'someone elses'! None of them did it to me. Not even my . . . husband! Only you."

"Ah, your husband. You said you'd married soon after high school. What happened? Did you divorce?"

She drew back slightly. "We're not . . . married anymore, that's true."

"For how long?"

"Eighteen months, but—"

"Eighteen months." That seemed to enlighten him, ease his mind. His tone grew cajoling. "Look at it as a healthy sign. You're becoming interested in men again. If I'm responsible, I suppose I'll have to take credit. But you can't mean to act out this impossible scenario of yours, and even if you do, I won't cooperate."

"No. You don't like to be pushed. Good men don't."

"Gayle, a man who works the kind of job I do is more likely to be bad than good."

"Maybe you're an exception."

He sighed again into a lengthening silence. The pianist sang on, memorializing *Des-per-ah-do,* a wary, weary man desperately afraid of his own emotions, especially desperation.

"So what do you want?" he asked bluntly. "You want me to sleep with you, is that it? Will you go away then?"

"You put it . . . plainly."

"That's the kind of man I am. I thought you knew."

"I want whatever you'll give me."

"Grief," he warned.

Her eyes met his squarely. "I've had grief before."

"Not my kind." Solitaire shifted restlessly. "This is ridiculous. I don't want you! Can't you understand the Queen's English? I won't be coerced by your mooning about. It's your money, your life. If you want to waste it, you're welcome to. Just don't waste my time."

Several quarters spun to the marble tabletop. As he stood to leave, the pianist caught his eye, smiled significantly and broke into a new song. Solitaire glared and stalked away, leaving Gayle to contemplate Solitaire's almost full rum and Coke and the lyrics of the new song that included his name.

By the time the chorus came, Solitaire was too far away

to hear it. But Gayle hummed the familiar melody, remembering the familiar words. And, as far as she was concerned, she was still in complete harmony with the song's sentiments. Solitaire was the only game in town.

She smiled sadly, sighed deeply, then rose and returned to the slot machine no one tried to claim anymore. She began pushing nickels down its throat, over and over, rhythmically, trying not to look toward the Baccarat Cove, trying to lose herself in the rhythm and the boredom until she didn't feel anything anymore, until she could go home to Canton, Kansas, the same functional, emotion-deadened woman who had left it.

Hours later, a shadow loomed over her. Hopefully, she looked up from her slot machine. It was only the tall dancer she'd seen talking to Solitaire, the one she'd accused him of having as a friend.

"Hi. My name's Darcy. What's yours?"

"Gayle. You don't waste time on introductions."

"I figure you don't have much time, Gayle. How's it going with our mutual friend?" Darcy hitched a sweatshifted shoulder in the direction of the baccarat area.

"He doesn't have any friends."

"Umm, progress. At least you must have got that line straight from the horse's mouth."

"He bought me a drink and told me to go to home or to go to hell, or as good as."

"Terrific!"

"Terrific?"

Darcy shrugged. "Boys are always mean at first to the girls they like."

Gayle's brown eyes darkened with anguish. "This isn't grade school, Darcy. This isn't a game. I don't play games; neither does he."

"I know. Look, Gayle, I don't know why you've decided Solitaire is the only star in your sky, but I know how it feels. I had to chase my husband like crazy until he finally decided to slow down and enjoy the race."

Gayle openly surveyed Darcy's statuesque form and glamorously made-up face. "Why? I'd think you could have anyone you wanted."

"Maybe, but I had to pick a shy man. Ooh, I liked him so much and wanted him so bad . . . but it worked out." Darcy flashed a discreetly sized diamond on her left hand.

Gayle pushed another nickel listlessly down the chute. She glanced rapidly to the Baccarat Cove and away again. "Solitaire isn't shy."

"No." Darcy fidgeted with the long braid that flipped over one shoulder. "No, he isn't. I don't know what he is. But he saved my life once, indirectly. Maybe I'd like to try to save his soul."

Gayle glanced up, struck by the seriousness with which the last words were said. "It's so crazy, I can hardly make myself believe it sometimes, but I love him, Darcy. I really do."

"That's kinda obvious." Darcy grinned again, devilishly. "And it's one thing our solitude-loving friend has never had to face before." She patted Gayle's shoulder. "I don't suppose he'll thank you for it, but love might be just what he needs. Keep the faith."

On her way out, Darcy paused again at the baccarat rail.

"Why don't you mind your business and go home?" Solitaire growled when he came over.

"Oooh! Touchy tonight."

"I saw you giving aid and comfort to the enemy."

"That sweet little thing? The enemy? I thought you could do better than that when it came to enemies."

"I can," he said flatly. "Apparently I could do better for friends too."

"You don't have any," Darcy said lightly. "I have it on the best authority. Well, I better get home to Steven and find out how Chapter Sixteen is going. Don't work too hard."

Darcy took three giantess-size steps away and paused to twist her face over her shoulder. "Sweet dreams."

Seven o'clock in the morning came to the Crystal Phoenix Hotel and Casino with no change in pace or lighting, only a sweeping change of shift among the employees.

In that sea-change, Solitaire once again ebbed quietly beyond the door marked Employees Only.

Gayle, poised with a nickel half in the slot, watched him vanish. She let the nickel join the scattering of coins in the pay-off bay. If she played right, Gayle could nurse the machine on nickels all night and break about even.

"Quittin' time, honey?" asked the purple-haired oldster who habitually worked the three machines next to Gayle's.

"I guess."

"You should play two or three at a time, better your odds."

"Thanks, but I'm afraid I'm a one-machine woman." Gayle began collecting her coins in a cup. Her back ached and her posterior had gone blessedly numb.

"*Hmph!*" The woman tilted a rouged cheek Gayle's way and winked into the deep crow's feet fanning across her cheekbones. "Play the percentages, honey! That's the only way to win in Vegas. Otherwise, you'll lose your sweet little ass."

Gayle's mouth dropped at the old lady's language. Tired, she yawned instead.

"See you tonight, sweetie," the old gal sang out as Gayle staggered through the casino in search of the elevators to her new room. "Same time, same station."

Gayle stopped. "How do you know?" she called back.

"The odds, kiddo. The odds."

In three minutes, Gayle was lurching down the hall of the seventh floor, looking for the room she'd never gone to. Seven-fifteen. She could hardly fit the key in the keyhole and leaned heavily against the door as it swung open, riding its impetus rather than her own.

Tired. Dead tired. It'd been over twenty-four hours since she'd slept. Her bags were there, as she'd ordered the bellman on returning to the hotel near midnight the evening before.

"You're crazy, Gayle."

She heard the phrase in Connie and Kelly's bemused voices when they realized that Gayle had been serious about turning right around and heading back to Las Vegas.

"Crazy."

Now the very walls of her new room seem to echo those sentiments.

"Raving mad," intoned a new voice in her mind.

She smiled. Australia, huh? At least Solitaire could say the same old thing with a different twist. Maybe that's what she liked about him, she thought, throwing herself fully dressed upon the made-up bed. One of the things. She was too tired to catalog the others, and slipped into a hard and dream-free sleep.

An endless drone of traffic on nearby Las Vegas Boulevard vibrated the walls of the Araby Motel. Farther north, the boulevard became the infamous "Strip." This near the airport it was just a street lined with sleazy motels, pawn shops, fast-food joints and the odd, garish wedding chapel.

In his room, atoss on the worn, once-gaudy bedspread, adrift in the drawn-curtain semi-dark of his daylight sleeping shift, Solitaire turned in a state that was not quite sleep.

They worried at him, the imps of introspection of a solitary life loose upon its subject. They nipped and harried and pinched and herded his semiconscious thoughts into one, unwelcome mass.

Friends. Did he have . . . friends? No, he was the perfect cipher, the complete nonentity. An emotionless zero. He'd lived that way, had schooled himself to live that way, for almost twelve years now—out of necessity.

Surely one self-deluded and determined young woman from Kansas couldn't be right, couldn't have seen something he had neglected to notice. He noticed everything. He had to. He couldn't have made the mistake of making friends . . .

Damn her, he thought, the anxiety jolting him fully awake. Sweat lay mist-like on his skin, clammy and unwelcome. Damn her for ruining everything. He'd stayed too long, he knew that now. Longer than anywhere else. Long enough to have attracted her single-minded attention. And if hers, why not someone else's?

Why? He'd never lingered overlong anywhere else before. Why at the Crystal Phoenix? Did he love his eighteen-karat gold watch and velvet coat, his false persona of authority that much? Or . . .

Friends.

The word coiled in his mind like a serpent, bringing a bitter expression to his usually impassive features. Friends. *Damn them.* And damn Darcy, with her well-meaning teasing—if only she knew what harm she did! What harm they all did, the ones who wanted to like him despite his best efforts to make himself unlikable. No one had aspired to love him before, but she was mad, Miss Kansas Cornfield, and half admitted it herself.

Crazy, crazy female. She was driving him into a corner, forcing him to run again. To leave Las Vegas, and the Phoenix and all the people he'd come to know there, that he'd come to regard as—there it was, in the open, the snake coiled to strike, its maw agape between the portcullis of lethal incisors—there was the word again, coming at him with the speed of a cobra's strike. Friends. They'd destroy him, these friends.

Love her? He hated her, with her wholesome buttermilk skin and brown velvet eyes—trusting eyes, eyes well suited to friends and such intangibles as love. She didn't know what she played with, how dangerous he could become if cornered, how tightly she was driving him into the dead end of his own emotions.

Solitaire stared at the ceiling, at the same blistered patch of peeling paint he always stared at. There was only one remedy—get rid of her. Once and for all. And he knew just how to do that. It was cruel, but he could be cruel in his own defense. Sometimes the deepest kindness wears a cruel face, he reflected.

♠ Chapter Five ♠

"You'll never get anywhere concentrating on one machine all by its lonesome like that, honey."

Exasperated, Gayle glanced at her gambling partner.

After three uneventful nights on slot machine duty, Gayle hadn't gotten close enough again to Solitaire Smith to distinguish him from his brother referees. Her right arm ached constantly, and her fingertips had grown numb. It was five o'clock in the morning of the third night, and she had lost about ninety-five dollars in nickels.

While Gayle doggedly pumped single nickels into her slot, Hester Polyester pushed nickels by the fistful down the three machines she monopolized and offered free, which is to say, unwanted advice.

It didn't help that Hester Polyester's advice could as easily apply to Gayle's romantic quest as to her gambling idyll. The racket was unnerving, but Hester apparently enjoyed setting up shop nearby simply so she could needle Gayle, who made a perfect sitting duck.

"You got to risk money to make money," Hester was declaiming now, her purple head nodding so soberly she resembled a lecturing iris in a Wonderland garden of talking flowers. "One nickel at a time won't get you much of a ride."

A hail of nickels hitting metal drew Gayle's attention back to her momentarily neglected machine.

Solitaire Smith, in the velvet-coated flesh, had materialized beside her and was beginning to ram nickels into her slot. Two, three, four, five. His hand paused on the chrome handle. "May I?"

Gayle assented with a nod, watching while he jerked the handle, hard. The three columns rotated wildly, flashing cartoon fruit past Gayle's eyes. Cherries came up in the left row and snapped to a smart stop in the middle. Amazed, she held her breath, but the third row produced only an out-of-sequence bell.

Two winning cherries multiplied the investment, however, so nickels chimed atop one another into a self-propagating pile at her knees. Gayle stared wordlessly, first at the mounting nickels, then at Solitaire Smith.

"Sometimes you have to show these things who's boss," he said without a softening smile. "All right. You win. On both scores. Tonight? Or should I say this morning?"

"What?" she demanded.

Hard green eyes darkened to malachite. "What you claimed you . . . want," he said softly.

"My place or yours?" She congratulated herself on sounding as blasé as he.

"Mine. I'll stop by for you for . . . breakfast."

She stared at him, her stomach sinking as fast as her temperature was rising. It hadn't seemed real until now, until he said yes. She would finally be within real reach of the man she so desperately wanted. She'd be able to touch that fascinating face, stare openly into his evasive green eyes, breathe her tremulous kisses onto those self-contained lips. The thought suddenly petrified her.

"Second thoughts?" he asked quickly, a bit triumphantly.

"No." She met his eyes. "First thoughts. Coming back hard."

His smile was slight and slightly cutting. "Shameless hussy, aren't you, Kansas?"

"No, but sometimes I can be if I have to."

"And when you've got what you think you want, you'll go?"

"When I've got what I want," she agreed, knowing he'd never believe what she really wanted. "Would it be . . . pushy if I changed my dress?"

"When did you start worrying about being pushy?"

"All my life."

His eyes grew thoughtful. Then his hand shot out to rumple her softly cropped hair. "Poor Kansas. Just remember. Sometimes we get what we want, and it's bloody hell."

She watched him fade back into the baccarat area, feeling as if someone had forced a double shot of brandy down her throat, tingling dizzily from fingertip to toe.

"Hester! Will you save my seat if I let you play my machine? I'll be back in forty-five minutes."

"Sure thing, sweetie." The old woman cackled, shifting her polyester derrière to Gayle's stool. "Nothin' I like better'n a warm stool—unless it's a hot machine. Sure you want to leave a winning slot?"

"I've got to!"

"Okay, never let it be said that Hester Polyester is one to stand between a girl and a good lay."

"Hester! You talk like a truck driver!"

"Why not? I was married to one for forty-nine years. So I know a good deal when I see it, which I didn't see very often with Chester, my husband, let me tell you."

"Some other time," Gayle hedged, fleeing with cups of nickels to change into bills before she could change herself.

Finally in her room, she stood before the glaring mirror, under the merciless fluorescent lights. She shook her soft, gleaming hair into the unsophisticated shape it took naturally. She brushed her teeth as if her life depended upon it. Fresh lipstick tinted trembling lips. She hesitated at blotting off the seductive gloss, but men hated lipstick smudges, and she imagined that they'd be doing plenty of smudging . . .

Her knees buckled, in turn. Gayle grasped the marble sink with both hands and tried to think logically.

They'd likely walk to his place, wherever it was, she decided, kicking off her high heels. She didn't want to have to mince after him like someone impaired. Most men hated feminine trappings that made women nonfunctional. So on with her beige mid-heel sandals, even if they did nothing for her ankles. Maybe Solitaire wasn't a leg man, anyway.

She stripped to her underwear, a new peach set trimmed with lace in all the right places. What *did* he like, this stranger she'd set her heart on?

Maybe she didn't possess anything he liked. Her waist wasn't small enough, her bust wasn't big enough, and her legs weren't long enough, she thought in panic. Why had she eaten that banana split in the Kansas City airport before flying back? Daytime, they'd be meeting in daytime. She traded her dressy aqua-crepe dress for a coral-silk blouse and cream-colored skirt.

Her fingers shook as she tried to slip her best gold and turquoise ear studs into her lobes. The tiny pullback latch on the matching chain and pendant refused to open until the fifth try.

She grabbed her purse and headed for the door. It was nearly six a.m., for heaven's sake, only an hour to go. Reversing course, Gayle flew back to the bathroom to envelop herself in a mist of sprayed scent—White Shoulders.

At the door she paused, looked back and took a deep breath. She would return to this room a changed woman. She could hardly wait.

Solitaire came and stood mutely beside the slot machine at seven-ten. Gayle jumped up, too fast, feeling like Don Knotts playing a nervous jack-in-the-box.

"Ready?" he asked.

"Yes," she lied.

They made their way out of the hotel into the still-crisp, late-March morning air. He wore comfortably casual clothes like she'd seen at breakfast three days ago. Solitaire kept mum on her change of clothing, her sensible shoes, her extravagant fog of perfume.

Instead he said, "You should have worn a jacket."

"I'll warm up walking."

He didn't answer, and Gayle paced him, feeling eager and uneasy, like a dog that doesn't know quite where it's going and must let its master lead.

"Are we stopping to have breakfast—first?" she asked as they passed the Dunes.

"I don't eat breakfast, remember?" Silent, she did. "Besides"—he shot her a quick, disquieting glance—"*you're* breakfast."

"And I suppose *you're* the big, bad wolf. Too bad I didn't wear my little red riding hood!"

He didn't answer. Strangers shouldered past them on the crowded sidewalks. She wondered what kind of couple they made in those indifferent eyes. Solitaire's easy attire and equally casual pose blended with the Western surroundings. Gayle's dressy clothing and uneasy attitude screamed "tourist."

They made an unlikely couple, she concluded, an even unlikelier one had the passerby known that they were en route to a romantic rendezvous—or should she consider it a tawdry one-morning stand? Gayle didn't quite know how to phrase it in her own mind. She huddled her arms around her midriff as the post-dawn wind rippled the silk blouse across her skin. Her icy hands sheltered under her elbows.

"I won't let you scare me off," she volunteered.

His hand on her arm stopped her in mid-stride.

"Give it up, Gayle," he argued, his features tight with what? Weariness? Compassion? "Go back to Oz on the next balloon out of this hellish town. You've caught gambling fever, though you don't know it. Go back while you still can."

When she was silent, staring into the wind and his face until mock tears stung her eyes, his fingers tightened on the soft flesh of her arm. "You can't take what I have to give, you know that."

"Yes, I can!"

He let his hand fall away and started walking again.

She scurried to catch up. "Where are we going?"

"Where I live. You wanted to come into my life, didn't you?"

"Not your life, exactly. I just want you."

"The life I lead *is* me, but you wouldn't believe that. You'll simply have to learn that for yourself."

"Solitaire." She stopped, letting him move ahead. He finally stopped and turned, impatient. "You're *punishing* me for caring about you, aren't you?"

He came back for her, step by deliberate step, moving like the bullfighter he had reminded her of, the first night she saw him.

"I'll walk you back to the hotel."

"No!"

He shrugged and started forward again. This time she joined him without comment, without question. With diabolical directness, Solitaire led her straight to the Araby Motel.

Primer-patched cars and trucks sank onto their bald tires before battered motel-room doors. Debris drifted across the parking-lot asphalt to the rhythmic prodding of the desert breeze. Somewhere on the second story, an infant squalled. Elsewhere, a radio played too loud.

Gayle stood beside him while he unlocked his door. He pushed it open on its squeaking hinges and waited gallantly while she preceded him into the room.

Gayle moved into blurred dusk, into a cube of drab dimensions, her shoes scuffing matted carpet that had barely held a nap when it was new. Behind her, the door shut with a final rasping sound. A chain lock ground into place.

"Home sweet home," Solitaire announced bitingly.

He rustled around the dim room, finally touching a lamp and sending a magic circle of light spilling over the bureau.

Gayle surveyed cheap Danish modern furniture from the Fifties: chair, nightstand and bed frame, their blond finishes caramelized with decades of cigarette smoke. Oval burn marks pocked the bureau rim and randomly scarred the forest-green carpeting. A doorless closet held a minimum of clothes. A gaping door opposite it indicated the shuddersome presence of a bathroom Gayle hoped she wouldn't have to use. Air stale as yesterday infected the atmosphere like rotten incense.

Solitaire, not moving now, watched her study the room. "They do change the sheets every morning."

She spun to face him. He had paused in front of the sagging drapes.

"Happy, honey?" he inquired in mock bridegroom tones.

She stared at his figure for mute seconds, then surprised herself by striding purposefully for the door.

Solitaire got there before her, holding her close against the rough denim that clothed him, his eyes mirroring the empty shadows in the room, his mouth moving angrily.

"Give the disappointed man a fond, farewell kiss before you go—and give my regards to Kansas!"

Behind her, his right hand was undoing the chain lock, dropping it back against the deep gash its weight had etched into the wood. Before her, his face was drawing close, his lips finally touching hers with a hard, resentful kiss.

His hand wrenched the doorknob, then pulled the door ajar. A widening sliver of daylight knifed into the dim room, staining their entwined figures with its slow, revelatory suffusion.

Gayle sensed all that at the same instant, seemingly, absorbed through a fog of horror and hurt. Talk about being "kissed off." She felt the coiled tension in his body, at last so close to hers, so unwelcome where it once was invited.

His mouth pressed hers in a parody of passion. And yet, as the taking force of him met the giving strength of her, a spark touched tinder. She hardened, and he softened. His hold upon her became less demanding, more desperate. Her body, seconds before stiffened into rejection, strained toward his with an answering intensity.

With her free arm, she slammed the door shut again, entombing them in murky twilight isolation. Her hand flailed behind her head for the free end of the chain to finish sealing them into this room that they both hated.

She found the brass slide and slammed the chain lock closed, producing so loud a ring of metal on metal that their eyes involuntarily flicked to the swaying loop of chain planing the worn wood.

Solitaire wrenched his mouth free. "Get out of here," it

ordered, pled. "Go home!" His eyes waged the opposite argument.

"I *am* home," Gayle insisted breathlessly, wrapping her free arm around his shoulders, curling her hand over the back of his neck and pulling his mouth toward hers, frightened by her own intensity. She could no longer speak or think. A series of low moans, hers, stopped only when his mouth met hers again.

If she had forgotten who he was and who she was, or what had led them to these timeless moments of shattering encounter, Solitaire hadn't. Yet for once, he took his own room for a haven, not a mocking hidey-hole. He was in the dark, behind his locked door, as usual, doing something unusual he knew he shouldn't be doing.

He had done only what he should, only what he dared to risk doing, for twelve years. Caution flew to the corners of his ugly, empty room, caged there for once while he reveled in unexpected freedom. Freedom was the faint taste of lipstick on his tongue, the deeper taste of excitement decanted from her lips.

Freedom was Gayle's blind, defiant relocking of the door, unlocking him from years, months, weeks, days, hours, minutes, and seconds of self-restraint.

Freedom was making love, finally, the way he needed to make it, hard and fast, without worrying about anything other than what he felt and how he needed to feel it.

He took her to the bed, prying open the tightly tucked bed linen as he would a clam, to expose the priceless pearl of clean sheets in such a dirty world. Gayle, once disinclined to drop so much as a shoe in this room, felt her clothes peel away like Band-Aids, with a stinging sense of discomfort too fleeting to name.

He came to her like a Kansas cyclone, announced but

still somehow unexpected, dark, twisting, and inexorable.

He left like an aftershock, ebbing silently away into no-longer fresh sheets, retracting his touch, the inflexible eye of his storm, his solitary satisfaction.

Reason, stealthy and sheepish, reclaimed them both. And regret, disappointment, a cloak of shame wide enough to shelter two.

Separately.

"This must be yours."

Solitaire, dressed, bent to the dark matted rug and a small gleam winking upon it. He surfaced with a silver heart-shaped pendant on a thin, broken chain.

"Yes." She finished buttoning her blouse and pulled the corpse of her purse across the rug by its shoulder strap.

"It must have broken when we—" he suggested.

"Yes," she agreed again, tonelessly. "A jeweler can fix it." She let the chain coil into an inside purse pocket and zipped it shut.

"I'll walk you back," he offered when she stood and stared at the door as if she'd never seen it before.

"No. You must be"—her sentence required a last word she was unwilling to say—"tired."

His expression wearied with more than fatigue. "You could take the bus, I imagine. It doesn't run often, but—"

"I'll walk. I like to walk."

"Do you?"

His eyes had recovered their mockery, but she met them anyway. It was hard to look at a man who had been both your lover and your ex-lover in the space of an hour.

"I don't regret it," Gayle said hastily.

"Thank you." He could still be sardonic.

"You were right." Her eyes lowered as she tucked in her wrinkled blouse and looked around for the excuse of more fallen bits of her attire. "I didn't understand. I"—only the wrong words would come to mind. "I've got to go."

He rose, glided through the dusk to the door, and unlocked it. He waited before it, his hand on the knob ready to release her into daylight, the chain weight rocking back and forth like a dolorous pendulum above his shoulder.

"Well . . ." Gayle settled her purse strap on her shoulder like a departing lady of affairs. "Good-bye."

"You're going back to Kansas?"

She nodded, her tousled hair shimmying.

"I didn't want to—" he reminded her.

"I know. I know." She took the knob in her own hand, his flying away from her impending touch, and twisted it. She squeezed through the door as soon as space permitted, not looking back.

"Good-bye," he said to the dark side of the door as its askew weight drew it closed. He shut it quietly, carefully, and locked it.

Arranging her inner self outside the door, Gayle heard the bolt turn, heard the chain knell itself home. She shivered in the sunshine, squinting toward the pock-marked sign announcing the Araby Motel's "reasonable rates."

She began walking the long blocks back to the Crystal Phoenix, watching toy-colored cars stream past her. Her muscles snapped like bubble gum. She would be sore by tonight, she thought, promising herself a hot bath as soon as she returned to the hotel. She wasn't used to making love like a . . . wild woman.

Gayle managed a smile as faint as Solitaire's usually was. She wasn't used to making love, period, anymore. It had been eighteen months, after all. What a comeback. The

Kansas Kid goes ten rounds with the Lone Stranger and loses on a technicality.

It wasn't the tawdry setting that had defeated her, the repressed passion that had attacked her from the first sound of the starting bell. It wasn't that Solitaire Smith had set out to prove himself right and her wrong, had intended to frighten her and had meant to wage love instead of make it all along.

It was that there was no love in him to liberate. She had beaten past his defenses and found only a great black hole, sucking all her good intentions into its pitiless maw.

"Live and learn," she told herself grimly, aloud, as she walked. "Live and learn. And listen to the man. Go back to Kansas, kid, before you get hurt."

Nothing looked the same, though. Everything looked cheaper and more artificial. Even the sun sparkling off the greenhouse roof on the hotel's Crystal Promenade highlighted the dull gleam of rare rain spots.

In the lobby, people milled as usual, and an expensively bleached blonde leading a white cat on a gold leash harangued the bell captain while the black house cat eyed the indifferent Persian.

Gayle sighed, her eyes automatically going to the Baccarat Cove. She cringed at glimpsing a man in a burgundy jacket. She could leave the hotel by three and be home by eight if she called the airline right away, she told herself.

Someone waved from the corner of her eye, a hazy blob of purple and pink. She didn't have the heart to say good-bye to Hester Polyester. At least there was one person in Las Vegas who might miss her a little, Gayle thought, moving sluggishly for the elevators.

She avoided the eyes of the lone man on the elevator, feeling that her . . . disarray would show, and pressed her floor number, seven. The round white button didn't light up. She leaned forward and pressed it again. Nothing happened, but the elevator doors opened on the mezzanine level.

"I think there's something wrong with the controls," Gayle started to tell the business-suited man who stepped on. "I can't press my floor—"

Hands caught her from behind in a close embrace, hands harder than Solitaire's had been, less careful, and that was saying something.

"Let go of me!"

"Not until you sing the words and music," a man's voice hissed at her ear.

Gayle rolled beseeching eyes at the businessman. He was fiddling with the controls but turned with an expression she could only describe as mean, like the smile on the face of a boy who's thinking about tearing the wings off a moth.

"What do you want?" she asked worriedly.

"We've seen you with Smith. All we want is his home address. That's all."

She twisted to view her captor, but his hands tightened and pain burned through her arm.

Gayle moaned. It didn't sound much different from her moans earlier that morning. She shuddered at the idea of two such extreme events occurring in the same day.

"What do you want him for?"

"Not for what you do, honey!" A hard chuckle behind her ended in a grunt. Gayle felt her forearm twist; it seemed to buckle. She would have screamed, but the other man clamped a hand over her mouth. An acrid drift of sweat reeked into her nostrils. Her head thrashed, feeling smothered.

"Shut up! Shut up, or you'll never see the seventh floor again."

So they knew her room number. Knew she knew Solitaire.

"Where!" the man was saying, his knee pushing painfully into her lower back, even while he pulled her arms in the other direction.

"I don't know! I don't, really! Please—"

The second man, the man who had stood by watching, who looked so respectably dressed, who probably had a room here at the Crystal Phoenix and had never stayed at a dump like the Araby Motel, hauled back his arm and hit her hard across the mouth.

That startled her, pained her more than anything that morning, the jolt of her own teeth into her inner lip, the thick taste of salt pooling over her teeth, the sickening snap of her neck from the blow.

"I don't, I don't—!" was all she could think to say.

She would betray him, give him away as he had thrown her away. She would have, only the words seem to have been shaken out of her skull by the blow, the words that would release her and destroy him. Why couldn't she find them? Why couldn't she say them? She wasn't a heroine in a thriller, and he wasn't a hero worth defending. He'd probably have stood mockingly by and advised her to say them himself, had he been here . . .

He wasn't here. No one was here but she and the two men who weren't afraid to hit women. Solitaire had never hit her, even though she felt as if he had after he'd finished making love—or whatever he called it.

"Come on, that pretty blouse is gonna get all stained if you don't talk fast. Look, we've got a nice white handkerchief here for your mouth. All you have to do is tell us where Smith hangs out. Then we're gone and, bingo, you're on floor seven and on your way to your own private bathroom to tidy up nice and neat again."

"I—" Gayle didn't know what she was going to say. She could feel a slow rivulet of hot drool edging out the corner of her mouth.

The elevator doors sprang open.

She was weaving on her feet, released as suddenly as she had been seized. A man in a maintenance uniform was beaming at her, then he turned to a white-haired couple behind him.

"Thanks for reporting this. There were some folks stuck on the elevator already. I'm sure it's working now. You want to stay in the same car, miss?"

"Uh, no. No. I think I'll walk."

The maintenance man grinned tolerantly and extended a hand to help her off the elevator. Gayle took it, needing it more than he knew.

"Sorry if you've been upset. Give me your room number, and the management will send up a complimentary gift."

"Uh, no . . . no, thank you. I'm fine. It was nothing."

Gayle swallowed a warm trickle of blood. In the hallway mirror, she looked amazingly fine. Her palm clutched something. A white handkerchief. Apparently the thug thought she'd look more natural carrying it than he. She started to giggle. The two men stood grimly at the back of the elevator, their eyes fixed on the floor numbers above the door as the elderly couple entered the car.

The doors started to slide shut. Gayle unfurled the hankie and waved it, still laughing hysterically.

"You sure you're okay?" The maintenance man's concern brought her back to reality.

"Yes, but is there a ladies' room on this level?"

"You look awful shook up, miss. Come on, I'll take you down to a private office. You can use the biffy there."

"That's . . . wonderful of you!" Gayle meant it, realizing that he had just promised her sanctuary. The men would never find her if she disappeared into the private areas of the hotel.

"We at the Crystal Phoenix don't like our guests put out, Miss," the man explained, leading her down an escalator to the main floor again. "I'll just take you back to the offices, and don't you feel you have to leave until you feel right about it."

"I won't," Gayle promised giddily. "I assure you that I won't."

♠ Chapter Six ♠

Gayle's knuckles tightened around the telephone receiver. Their icy coldness soothed the tender heat of her struck cheek.

"I don't care if you don't think he's in," she repeated. "Knock until he answers; I know he's there. This is urgent."

Gayle waited tensely as the phone line hung open in extended silence. The manager of the Araby Motel had spoken in slurred disinterest, loath to trudge the few feet to Solitaire's door. Of course the Araby Motel didn't offer a phone in every room, any more than it did a TV set. Its sign had even listed an additional daily rate for color TV.

Maybe the man had abandoned the open line, she fretted as the minutes passed, had left her dangling. Gayle absently studied the empty office she'd retreated to. She'd drawn the blinds, so it was hard to see. Color prints of ballerinas and wild animals defined the grass-cloth walls, a young woman's environment, Gayle surmised, a young woman who was vacationing somewhere, never dreaming that her office was playing a set for a tawdry soap opera . . .

"Yes?" This male voice sounded as put-out as the manager's, but infinitely more energetic.

Gayle jumped, having been lulled by the manager's indifference into expecting nothing, now startled by a response.

"It's Gayle."

His silence rebuked her. Her rising pride joined him. She hated Solitaire thinking that she would call him after what had happened between them.

"I hope I didn't wake you, but I had to warn you," she said baldly. "When I got back to the Crystal Phoenix, some men . . . detained me. They wanted to know where you lived. They wanted to make me tell them where you lived."

"Did you?"

"No." She didn't want him to think she cared enough to save him. "It happened on a stuck elevator. A maintenance man interrupted us."

"That's all?"

"Isn't it enough?" Her anger and bewilderment merged briefly.

"Where are you now?"

"In an empty office in the hotel administration area. The maintenance man brought me here to clean up. I'm sure the men don't know where I am, but they did seem to know my room number—or the floor, anyway."

"Clean up?" He pounced on just the wrong two words.

This time *she* kept silent for long seconds. "They, um, wanted to know where you were, awfully bad." She wouldn't tell him they had hit her. You don't tell a man who's hurt you in one, invisible way that you can be hurt in other, more obvious ways.

"How bad?" Calm, flat, inexorable. His voice was as apt an attribute as his tailor-made nickname, Gayle realized.

"They hurt me," she finally admitted tonelessly, "a little. But I'm leaving town in a few hours. You . . . you'd better watch out, that's all I called to say."

A disconcerting silence made the phone sound as if it held its mechanical breath, finally forcing Gayle to say another thing she had wanted to avoid articulating, his name.

"Solitaire?"

"I'm thinking."

The silence lengthened. Gayle rubbed her swelling cheek. It felt golf-ball-size to her fingertips.

"All right." His voice revived, crisp, commanding. "Stay

there. I'll come by in an hour."

"That's crazy! The men are here, looking for you!"

"The hotel's the last place they'll look for me until it's my shift. Why else would they have bothered with you? Do as I say."

"Why should I? I'm leaving Las Vegas, just like you wanted. I'll make sure I don't ride any elevators alone, that's all. You don't have to bother with me anymore—"

"Shut up." He meant it.

Gayle opened her mouth to protest, felt her jaw throb, and subsided.

"Stay there," Solitaire was saying in a high-handed, decisive tone that meant business. "Is there a nameplate on the desk?"

"Uh"—she felt among the stacked papers—"Lucy. Lucy Wrightson."

"Stay there. I know where you are. I'll come. An hour."

The line clicked dead. Gayle swung one foot, idly kicking the side of the desk. She didn't have to do what he told her. She'd gone out of her way to do him a favor, and now she should leave. Why should she stay? Just because he'd told her to? Why should she do anything he said?

Gayle let the buff-colored business phone slip into its cradle. Someone passed in the hall beyond the closed office door. Her body stiffened. She was frightened, Gayle admitted to herself. She was almost frightened enough to do what Solitaire said, even if it meant doing something that scared her more than anything—seeing him again.

An eternity passed before someone paused at the office door once more. In it, Gayle felt her wrist and cheek swell and her expectations flatten.

The door finally cracked open. She started as someone slid in and shut it again.

"No one's bothered you?" Solitaire asked quickly.

"Except you."

He ignored her spontaneous jibe and moved around the office's perimeter, scouting it like a dog. He wore beige camouflage-style pants and shirt, bristling with self-important pockets on legs and sleeves—a Beverly Hills globetrotter chic oddly out of character—and a down vest.

"What did they look like?" he wanted to know.

"Two ordinary businessmen. Medium height, medium hair, clothes, everything."

"One didn't have a receding hairline with a scar high over the left temple?"

"No, no one like that."

"American?" he interrogated next.

"Definitely." Amazed, Gayle watched Solitaire rifle any file and desk drawers he passed in his exploratory excursion around the room. "Should you be doing that?"

He straightened and looked her in the eyes for the first time since he'd entered the room. His expression, which in her imagination had assumed many bizarre and rather frightening forms, registered taut amusement.

"Might be something I can use, that's all."

"You're good at finding things like that," she riposted bitterly.

"No, they usually find me." He leaned against the desk a few feet from where she perched on it.

Gayle sighed. "Who are these men?"

"Killers."

"My God!" She let her feet hit the floor, as if to run. "Who do they want to kill?"

"Me. And anyone who gets in their way getting to me."

"Why?" she breathed.

"If they're here, I can't stay," he mused, ignoring her

question. "We'll have to leave tonight."

"Killers." Gayle felt dazed. She'd been penned in the hands of killers and Solitaire wouldn't tell her why. Maybe he was right. She didn't want to know. "I'm leaving as soon as I can book a flight, so I'm no problem to them. And if you leave the Araby Motel—"

"I've left. But you can't go back home. You've got to go with me."

"With you! Why? Of course I'm going home, why the hell not?"

Solitaire picked up a brass letter opener and weighed it as if he were contemplating its usefulness as a weapon.

"Because they'll follow you. They saw us together here. They've never seen me 'with' a woman before. They've decided you can lead them to me. The tragic part is they're half bloody right. So if I disappear, they'll follow you back to Kansas and hurt you until you tell them where I am."

"But . . . I won't know!"

"By the time they realize that, they'll have to kill you," he said matter-of-factly. "So you're safer, if you can call it that, going with me."

"I won't! I wouldn't go with you to the Laundromat! Besides, if you're so worried about my safety, aren't you making it worse by forcing me to go with you?"

He shrugged. "Could be. But I've eluded them for twelve years."

"Twelve years?" Despite herself, Gayle edged closer. "But . . . why?"

He threw the letter opener like a dart. It vibrated into the wall-mounted corkboard across the room before its weight pulled it free and to the floor.

"I don't know," Solitaire said, meeting her look head-on. He had slumped, half-sitting on the desk, so their eyes were level. "That's one thing I've never been able to figure out. But they've been trying to do it for twelve years. Not always the same hired killers. This sounds like a new lot."

"Why don't you go to the police?"

"I have. I've gone to the police on three continents. They don't believe me. It's damned difficult to make them when one can't produce a single reason for why someone is trying to kill him. And then, going to the police leaves a most legible paper trail. I don't go to the police anymore."

"Then maybe you're wrong. Maybe they're not trying to kill you. Maybe someone owes you money or—"

"They killed a woman," he interrupted. "A woman in Cape Town. Who knew me." He reached to take Gayle's frozen-featured face in his hand, tilting it up to the harsh fluorescent lights. "They hurt her first, and then they killed her. She didn't know where I was either." His thumb suddenly stroked her cheek, and she flinched. "You'll live. Is that all they did?"

"Pretty much." Her aching arm and strained back hardly seemed worth mentioning now. "But I don't *want* to go with you," she complained dully, still disbelieving.

His hand dropped from her face, the thumb lightly feathering down her throat in the gentlest touch he'd ever given her. "What a difference a day makes," he noted sardonically. "Is everybody in Kansas as much of a weathervane as you?"

"No, just the natural-born idiots," she accused herself angrily, stepping back from him and the lump that had knotted her throat for no reason.

Solitaire's expression hardened, if that were possible. He stared at the print of a wild boar on the opposite wall.

"I didn't want you," he said softly. "I didn't want you yesterday, and I don't want you today. But it's too late for that. What's real is them. Not you, not I, and not what either of us wants. It's taken me twelve hard years to learn that."

He looked at her again, with anger. "You'll come with me whether you want to or not. You'll come with me because I refuse to let you die, just as you refused to let me live."

"I"—Gayle wanted to defend herself—"I didn't know."

"Now you do." He stood. "Come on. We've got some shopping to do."

"Oooh, those boots are definitely 'you,' " the salesclerk bubbled. "They look super on."

Gayle stared at the four-hundred-dollar doe-colored eelskin boots on her feet. Standing among the nearby carcasses of a half-dozen tried-on boots, Solitaire stubbed his battered boot-toe at a lower-heeled fuchsia leather pair executed in classic cowboy style.

"She'll take those."

"A lovely choice, Sir. Although the eelskin are a bit more practical—the color, you know—these are most high-fashion. I'm sure your lady'll love them."

The clerk was sweeping boots into box when Solitaire spoke again. "She'll wear them."

Glaring, Gayle tugged on the boots while the saleswoman dumped her sensible beige sandals into a bag and headed for the cash register. Solitaire pulled out six hundred-dollar bills and, when he got the change, zipped it into a pocket in his down vest.

"You must have had some lucky streak in the casino, sir," the saleswoman trilled in smiling farewell. "How nice of you to share the wealth with your lady."

"Some lucky streak," Solitaire agreed flatly, taking

Gayle's arm and hustling her back into the Crystal Phoenix's indoor shopping arcade.

They'd already visited a fashionable boutique three shops down, where Gayle had exchanged her blouse and skirt for a pair of black Gloria Vanderbilt jeans and a suede-trimmed, Western-styled shirt. She wore both items now, at Solitaire's insistence. Shopping bags heavy with her discarded clothing hung from her hands. He'd also insisted she purchase several pairs of thick anklets emblazoned with trendy punk rock designs.

"You're crazy," Gayle hissed in his ear as they prowled the wide-aisle concourse. "I don't need this stuff. And where'd you get all that money?"

"I earned it," he said shortly, jerking her to a stop by an open storefront. "Obviously I didn't have much rent to pay.

"Sunglasses," he declared, twisting several pair off their display carousel and holding them up in turn to the fluorescent lights overhead. "These."

"At least let me try them on first to see if they fit!"

Gayle snatched the glasses from his fingers and thrust them onto her temples. The well-lit interior world of the shopping arcade went pitch-dark, then Solitaire whisked the sunglasses off her face and passed them with another hundred-dollar bill to the clerk behind the counter.

"This is insane," she protested again, in vain, for just steps ahead he pulled her to a stop in front of another fashionable women's clothing boutique.

This time his eye had snagged on a wooly white lambskin jacket with brushed suede sleeves in the display window. This time it took twelve hundred-dollar bills before Gayle left the store with the lambskin on her back, feeling anything but lamb-like.

"I don't need this," Gayle complained despite the people

93

milling around them. "You must have lost your mind."

Solitaire's ever-present hand remained clamped to her elbow as he guided her onto the escalator leading up to the hotel's main floor.

They dodged through a maze of clanking slot machines and finally through the forbidden door marked Employees Only.

" 'Lo, Solitaire," an armed security guard greeted them in passing.

Solitaire nodded curtly, but Gayle almost screamed for help. Before she'd made up her mind, Solitaire had steered her to a rear door and into the glaring sunshine outside, where a Dumpster as big as football's The Refrigerator waited open-mawed. While she watched, dazed, he wrenched the shopping bags containing her old clothes from her hands and discarded them.

"Oh—!"

He glanced at her. "Pickup's in a couple of hours. Once your clothes are in that dump truck grinder, no one will know you've left. No trail. That's the only way."

He led her back to the now-familiar office that belonged to Lucy Wrightson, who was lucky enough to be on vacation. Gayle had been on vacation once, she thought wistfully. On vacation in Las Vegas, where she had seen a man in a red velvet coat who had mesmerized her. . . .

Solitaire sat her down on the desk chair and quickly scanned the office landscape, as if hunting for changes.

"I don't need this stuff," Gayle protested again. What was he trying prove?

"You'll need it. It gets cold on the desert at night."

"The desert! Is that where we're going?"

"That's where we're going. And those baby-soft eelskin boots wouldn't have lasted one night on the desert. These cowhide ones we bought are built tough. The Gila monsters and whiptails don't care what color they are. Neither do I."

"The desert! Why should I go to the desert?"

"It's the only place I know how to survive," he said simply. "Alone."

"You're not going to be alone—"

"No." He didn't sound happy about it. "Are you hungry? What do you want to eat?"

"I—" Gayle realized she'd forgotten about food, about breakfast, lunch, and maybe even dinner, "I don't think I'll ever eat again."

"You'd better. You won't last the night if your body doesn't have any calories to burn. Unfortunately, it can't burn mute female fury."

"I'm not . . . furious! I'm not even angry with you."

"Why should you be? I thought you were infatuated with me."

"I was naive," she admitted.

"No argument. What do you want to eat?"

"Protein, I suppose, but where?"

Solitaire twisted his wrist to reveal the irony of his costly gold watch. "Three o'clock. Kitchen should be quiet between the lunch and dinner rushes. Chef Song should be out of the way and won't even notice what little we'll take. I can probably get enough to make a survival pack."

He turned at the door to say one final thing before leaving, but she anticipated him.

"I know. Stay here."

She thought about slipping away while he was gone, about returning to her room, making a plane reservation, and leaving anyway. But her right arm began throbbing in time to the ache in her jaw, and her back grew stiffer with every passing second. The men, she remembered, had just begun to question her when they were interrupted.

Gayle waited.

A figure finally came through the door, stooped and mis-shapen as Quasimodo. Gayle jumped up again, but the in-truder turned to lower a Santa-Claus-bulky-burden, a back-pack.

"Got a present for me?" she asked archly.

Solitaire tossed her a rectangle of sandwich in a plastic bag and set about inventorying his belongings on the floor.

"Roast beef," Gayle cooed happily, her mouth full, de-spite some tenderness. "I didn't know I was so hungry." She watched Solitaire, now loading the supposedly decorative pockets of his attire with matches and batteries, insect re-pellent, sun screen, and Band-Aids.

She eased off the desk and went to stand over him, her cheeks puffed out like a pocket gopher's, and not just from swelling. "Where'd you get that stuff, and what are you doing?"

"This is the kit I take on my desert hikes. I always keep it ready at the motel. For emergencies. I stashed it in my locker in the employee area before I came here. I'm repacking for two." He weighed an Ace Bandage in his palm, then rapidly assigned it to the smaller of the two backpacks. "You carry a comb in that purse of yours?"

"Of course." She hauled it out, ran it through her hair, and offered it to him.

He stuck it in one of the bags. "I didn't have grooming in mind," he noted. "If you have anything essential in your purse, transfer it to your pockets, or to one of mine. I can carry the backpack, but you'll have to manage the daypack." His thumb jerked to the smaller bundle.

Gayle hefted the weight by its canvas straps. "No problem," she assured him, her back tightening painfully as she lifted. "What'll I do with my purse?"

"Ditch it in the Dumpster." Solitaire was consulting a checklist of everything from chocolate bars to bullets. Gayle hadn't seen a gun yet, but most of the supplies had been prepackaged.

"What about my clothes and things, upstairs in my room?"

"They're goners, like most of my kit back at the motel. Maybe the hotel will hold them for you. If it's ever safe to come back. Try this."

He pulled a figured bandanna from the pack and tied it around his neck, handing Gayle one in a matching pattern.

"Gee, red for me, blue for you. I think that's sexist."

His hands poised impatiently at the blue knot at his neck. "You want this one?"

"Just kidding."

Solitaire stopped packing and leaned back on his heels to stare up at her. " 'Kidding,' " he commented wryly. "You appear to be rising to the occasion, Kansas. Must be the roast beef."

"When do we leave?"

"Dark," he answered. "When we can't be seen. There's more I'll need to scavenge. Should work well about six-thirty. That's usually a dead time back here."

Gayle winced. "I wish you wouldn't use that expression."

His dark eyebrows raised questioningly.

" 'Dead time.' "

"Apparently you're beginning to take our situation seriously."

"I always have."

They stared at each other until Solitaire let his assessing glance fall back to the items at his knees. "I've sure as hell left something vital out, but we should do fairly well."

Gayle made a noncommittal sound and returned to the desk chair, where she sat. "I have a feeling I'd better rest while I can."

At six-fifteen, Solitaire finally straightened and rose from the floor. "Come on. We'll leave this lot here while we make our last foray."

"Where?" she wanted to know, but he shushed her as he opened the door to the hall.

In moments he had led her down the deserted passage to another empty office. Farther down the corridor a door marked Van von Rhine, Manager swung ajar on darkness.

Solitaire pushed the light switch. Overhead fluorescent lights swelled into daylight brilliance.

"We should have brought the sunglasses," Gayle whispered, blinking and disoriented on the threshold.

Solitaire closed the door behind them and paced to the central lacquered desk topped with glass, big for a lady executive, searching its drawers.

"Solitaire! That's *her* desk. What are you looking for?"

"This!" He straightened triumphantly. "I saw it once, and knew it was in here somewhere."

"That's theft! And what is it, anyway?"

He unfolded a stiff accordion of white paper on the huge glass desktop. "An old map of the Mojave, over forty years old, a desert survival map drawn by old-timers who knew how to live out here when only sidewinders, scorpions, and centipedes did. It shows washes, secret springs, old trails and forgotten roads." The map rattled warning as he refolded it. "With this, we can elude a better-outfitted party."

"Won't things have changed since then?"

"Some. This is desert we're talking about. Water is rare, but it can flood the washes. Still, major landmarks remain." Solitaire spun to face the wall above the desk. "Look at that old black-and-white aerial photograph. It's over forty years old too. I wager if we flew over it today, the same landmarks would be there—the wash on the left, even that rock formation that looks like a camel."

"It does, doesn't it?"

Solitaire was shaking out the map again and staring at it. "Does what?"

". . . does look like a camel, that rock formation."

He jerked up his head to study the photo, then lowered it to the map again. "It bloody well does," he muttered. "Looks exactly a ruddy camel lost alone out on the desert."

"Lost on the desert, like us?" Gayle wondered.

Solitaire straightened with a grin that showed white teeth and made Gayle realize how deeply tanned his face was. Of course Solitaire would be one for lone desert hikes.

"What's wrong?" she demanded. "You're smiling."

"Was I? Sorry." The grin dissolved from his face as he refolded the map and jammed it inside the down vest. "Well. Ready?"

"Aren't you going to eat something too?"

"Not now. Not until we're away from here. Come on. I just remembered where we can get some wheels."

The "wheels" came on a dusty jeep in the hotel parking lot. It was painted powder blue. Solitaire slung their packs into the back, checked the Jeep's water supplies, and broke open the weapon box with a screwdriver. He lifted out a rifle and checked the chamber, grunting satisfaction.

"Sufficiently lethal, I presume?"

"Precisely. Get in, and I'll start the motor."

Starting the motor involved doing something under the blue hood, then returning to the driver's seat and hot-wiring something under the dashboard.

"Whose Jeep is this?" Gayle wanted to know as sparks

flew between Solitaire's oil-blackened fingers.

"Jill's," he grunted. "The small dark-haired woman who stops by sometimes. I'm sure you've seen her."

"The one with the baby?"

"Right."

"And you're taking her *car!*"

"It's hardly a 'car.' Besides, her husband is Johnny Diamond, the singer. He's got enough cars for six people. Jill won't be stranded." Solitaire paused in backing the Jeep out of its slot to grin once again. "But she will be furious."

"That's how you repay your friends? You rip them off? You break into your employer's office? I can see why you need the map, and it isn't valuable to anyone, but this . . . this is outright theft."

"Jill of all people would understand," he said grimly. "Besides, I told you. I don't have any 'friends.' "

"I can see why," Gayle observed.

The Jeep lurched onto the main boulevard and toward the black swallowing maw of the desert that lay cheek by jowl with the bright, glittering neon-white teeth of Las Vegas grinning in all its nighttime glory.

With air whistling through the Jeep's fragile ragtop, Gayle cringed into the cozy lambskin jacket, burrowing her hands into the pockets and wiggling her toes in warm but jazzy punk-rock socks inside her boots.

"Try this." Solitaire plunked a cowboy hat on her head. "It's Jill's," he added as she removed the hat to study it under the passing street lamps. "Funny that she left it. It's her trademark. Good thing, though. I forgot you'd need a hat. And Jill wouldn't want a tourist from Kansas to get her brains sun-scrambled on her desert, so consider it a loan in absentia."

"Thievery," Gayle answered unequivocally. "It's going to

get *hot* out there? I'm freezing."

"It's going to get hotter than you can imagine," he prom-ised, shifting gears as the Jeep accelerated to highway speed.

Gayle bounced on the high, hard seat, feeling sore mus-cles tense all over her body. Every jolt made her feel she'd been hit in the face again, and made her remember the physical bruising in the elevator and the emotionally bat-tering intensity of their morning assignation.

She slid onto her tailbone and tipped the hat over her eyes so the iodine-pink highway lights overhead wouldn't flash rhythmically into her eyes like amber warning lights.

"What a difference," she quoted a man of her acquain-tance, of her very slight but intimate acquaintance, "a day makes."

♠ Chapter Seven ♠

Midnight Louie Takes a Bum Rap

I see the happy couple ride off into the sunset from the window of my favorite suite, seven-thirteen.

All right, so it is more than somewhat past sunset when they depart in Mrs. Johnny Diamond's (nee Miss Jill O'Rourke) powder blue Jeep.

And, all right, so it is seven stories from the window of the suite to the parking lot and a few extra feet besides, but I am noted for my night vision. You could say it runs in the family.

And, all right, they seem more unhappy than happy, but that is to be expected when you mix unknown quantities of the opposite sex.

Nevertheless, I am as usual among the first informed of an unusual coming and, in this case, going in the Crystal Phoenix. I am not much concerned, as Mr. Solitaire Smith is a man after my own heart and it bothers me not one whit that he finds it expedient to . . . er, extract . . . certain items of a practical nature from certain areas of the hotel before he leaves.

There is honor among thieves, after all, and I am not about to blow the whistle on such a skillful member of the brotherhood, especially as he is obviously in a very sticky situation. And I am not talking about the little doll from Kansas, who is a sweet kid and all, but definitely looks like the type who would prefer dogs to cats—small, fluffy, black dogs, if you want my opinion.

So it does not surprise me that Mr. Solitaire Smith has to take it on the lam (no relation to the fuzzy, edible kind) or that he is admirably close-mouthed, as usual, while doing it.

What does surprise me is to witness two thugs of a falsely respectable nature sneaking out of Miss Gayle Tyson's hotel room that very evening. It is, of course, coincidental that her room is number seven-fifteen and adjacent to my own.

(I consider suite seven-thirteen my own for four reasons: it is vacant and never let; I enjoy the occasional nap on its definitely classy although somewhat dated premises; and thirteen is my lucky number, as well as my age. The last reason is actually two, so you see I have not forgotten my multiplication tables or anything, despite a certain maturity.)

What does surprise me happens the next morning, and it happens with a bang. The Old Nick is raised all around the Crystal Phoenix, and when some say Old Nick they mean the devil, but at the Crystal Phoenix when Nick of any nature is to be raised, young or old, it is always in the form of Mr. Nicky Fontana, the owner, my boss and a fine fellow on most occasions.

This bang occurs in the form of an explosion in the kitchens of Chef Sing Song, who discovers certain food stuffs of an unauthorized nature missing.

I am sorry to report that such is the predictability of human nature that my name is taken in vain. Naturally, I linger in the hallway shadows to eavesdrop and leave it to Mr. Nicky Fontana to defend me, who says like this:

"Now, Chef Song, you are a fine executive chef and the very soupbone of the Crystal Phoenix, but do not bestir yourself so vociferously. I am sure that our cherished resident feline and house detective, Midnight Louie, did not lay so much as a milk-white whisker upon your roast beef and the other missing edibles. So calm yourself and be assured that I shall immediately restore whatever is missing, and please refrain from casting aspersions upon one who is my bosom buddy as well as the heart and soul of the Crystal Phoenix."

Well, he says somewhat like that. I immediately retreat to the office of Miss Van von Rhine for a tea time treat to soothe my ruffled reputation. But she sees one hair of my revered hide and breaks out in a shriek that brings Mr. Nicky Fontana running.

Then she says like this, loudly:

"That impossible cat! Oh, Nicky, I hate to bother you with trifling complaints, but Jersey Joe Jackson's map is missing from my top drawer. I am planning on having it framed to match the aerial black-and-white photo from suite seven-thirteen, and I looked in my desk this morning and it is gone!

"It was there yesterday, my love, I swear upon my father's grave, and I just now see that admirable but somewhat light-pawed feline retreating down the hallway. Midnight Louie is prone, you know, to disport himself upon my desk and generally play havoc among my most intimate papers, so I have no doubt that he is the culprit in this case."

"You must be right, my delight," replies Mr. Nicky Fontana in sickeningly soothing tones. "Just now Mr. Sing Song finds several pounds of foodstuffs missing from his kitchen and I have no doubt that our resident example of avoirdupois is behind it all. Perhaps we can still find the rogue and wrest the map from his playful grasp. In the meantime I will take you to lunch at Nicky's Crystal Carousel topside and ease your distress with a fine bottle of French wine."

This speech has the desired effect, but there is nothing for me to do but slink away and reflect on the fickleness of human nature. Of course I am innocent and wrongfully accused with none to defend me.

I amble into the vicinity of Miss Savannah Ashleigh's suite on the seventh floor, tiring myself greatly on the stairs. So I cast myself into a heap at her service door, which is slightly ajar, and who should peek a piquant whisker through but the Divine Yvette, who greets me like this:

"Ah, Louie, *mon ami.* (The Divine Yvette tends to talk like this in moments of stress.) What is the matter? You look like something the dog dragged in. What troubles you? I could use an amusing tale of the streets, as my mistress has been most tiresome about her manicure today and has found a stale brandy truffle among the offering from her producer."

So I tell how I am falsely accused of nefarious activities in the Crystal Phoenix—my hotel that I am willing to give my very life to defend, or at least one or two of them!— and the Divine Yvette coos most consolingly through the crack in the door and pushes through a soft white pedicured appendage to pat gently at my ruff.

It is some consolation to stare into her unblinking pale-jade eyes so delicately edged in natural black and to hear her melodious humming under her breath as I speak. Truly, the Divine Yvette is living proof that even the sorest soul may find surcease at last.

And speaking of surcease, I devoutly hope that Mr. Solitaire Smith and Miss Gayle Tyson find nothing but brittlebush, rocknettle, sandpaper plant, prickly poppy—

and, ahem, catclaw—in the desert, which is purported to be in full bloom this time of year, as is hay fever of the most virulent nature.

♠ Chapter Eight ♠

"Oh no you don't! Not that tired old trick."

Gayle, exhausted and nerve-worn from too little sleep, too much stress, and two hours of jolting over uneven desert trails in pitch dark, could still dish up an ample serving of well-simmered indignation.

Solitaire paused in shaking open a sleeping bag on the crude dirt floor. The fire he'd built from gathered mesquite branches and lit with camper's combustible jelly and matches flickered bravely against the curved sandstone wall of the stone cabin.

Its feeble warmth seemed purely symbolic against the night's bone-freezing chill, but the flames flared bright enough to etch shadowed lines of worry into Solitaire's usually smooth features.

"There's only one sleeping bag," he pointed out patiently. "We need to conserve"—the innocent incitement of the next phrase struck him before he uttered it, and his eyelids flicked momentarily shut in recognition of that as he continued tonelessly—"body heat."

"I'll conserve my own, thank you."

"My, my . . . how times and tunes change."

"How they *are* changed, by other people's cruelty."

"I can't afford to be cruel now," he admitted after a moment. "Come on, Gayle, get in. You know you need sleep."

"You think crawling into that thing with you will help me sleep?"

"Warmth will help you sleep. Besides"—he reached up to grab the open lambskin jacket edges and begin tugging her

107

to the ground—"the scorpions can't get into it."

She shuddered, letting herself sink to her knees. Solitaire was pushing the jacket off her shoulders, a gesture too similar to one she would have welcomed twenty-four hours earlier.

"Lambskin's too bulky for sleeping in. You'll do better without it." Having explained himself, he unhanded her, allowing Gayle to shrug off the jacket herself.

"And your boots."

She sat to tug them off, finally leaning back on her hands while Solitaire wrenched them off and extended his booted feet in turn. Grunting, Gayle finally dislodged one, then the other, her back burning as if getting a hot-needle tattoo all over.

"All right," he said. "Slide in and tuck up."

She complied, her sore muscles welcoming the thin comfort of down, the very idea of being encompassed, even as her mind chaffed at the ironic implications of their sleeping arrangement.

Gayle rolled onto her sore side, facing outward, and waited for the jolting of the bag while he joined her. The zipper closed with a long grating noise. So far, nothing or no one had touched her. Her muscles relaxed.

"Are you hungry?" Solitaire's voice resonated from too near.

"No. And I'm not sleepy, either."

She watched the fire's faint shadows flicker over the reddish walls, like the ghost of a magic lantern show. The small semicircular room seemed like the inside of a red brick furnace, something cozy in its oven-like security.

In moments, after-images like smoky crimson tongues were etching their lurid dance on the inside of Gayle's shut eyelids. Seconds later, the dancing mirage merged with the ebb and flow of blood through her veins. Awash in waves of welcome heat, Gayle escaped into sleep.

Solitaire lay awake, his eyes searching the tiny cabin's perimeter for stirring scorpions. He'd tried to evict any desert creatures that had shared the same shelter, but the desert sand and its residents were stubborn: they always crawled or blew back into shelters no matter how rudely swept from human doors.

The floor felt ironing-board hard, but Solitaire, used to camping in desolate areas, could sleep on a slag heap. Beside him, curled into the farthest stretch of the sleeping bag, Gayle breathed in deep, tandem rhythm with the still-leaping flames.

An alley of mutual warmth was already burning between them, but he felt only ice within himself. Found again. Fleeing again—this time with an unwilling, unwanted companion. One fist clenched. Would it never end? It would never end until he could discover why it had begun. In twelve years he had never come close.

A soft, pained moan in the night. He twisted to see Gayle in the faint aura the firelight cast. Sweat shone like scattered seed pearls on her forehead. He unzipped the bag enough to lift her shoulders free.

"What's the matter?" he whispered, though there was little cause to whisper except the convention of night.

"I was sleeping," came the accusing drone of a sleep-sullen child.

"You moaned."

"I couldn't help it." Her voice remained slow, sleep-drugged.

"What hurt?"

"What doesn't?" She was awakening fully. "Everything hurts. First those men. Then that awful Jeep ride—it felt like Space Mountain at Disneyland! Now this rocky floor—"

"Here's some aspirin. Chew it."

"Aargh!" She tried to spit the tablets he pressed into her mouth back onto his fingers but they dissolved, stinging tartly, in her mouth.

"It won't kill you to take them dry. Now, where does it hurt the most?"

"My back." She groaned as he shifted her. "That thug really knew how to give a massage."

"Why didn't you tell me sooner?"

"One sore back didn't seem worth complaining about in view of what happened to that woman in Cape Town."

He was rolling her away from him and pulling up the shirt at the back of her waist.

"Hey! What are you doing?"

"Stay still! I've got to check the scene of the crime."

"In pitch dark?"

"I've got a flashlight handy."

"I bet you do."

"Unzip your jeans."

"Go fish!"

"I've been there, remember?"

Gayle tried to twist away, but her sudden buck cracked a whip of fire over her lower torso. She groaned and pulled down her zipper. Cool air hit her bared midsection. Solitaire's warm fingers rested on the curve of her waist, conferring a strange security in this alien, unseen pit of desert blackness.

A long low whistle pierced the night air. Gayle stiffened, her back regretting the impulse instantly.

But Solitaire wasn't admiring her Venus de Milo torso.

"You've got a bruise as big as my hand on your lower spine that would put an Arizona sunset to shame. It must hurt like hell."

She twisted onto her back again, away from his eyes and hands. "It does. *Ugh!* Maybe the aspirins will help. It's not like we can plug in a heating pad."

The flashlight clicked off, plunging them into deeper darkness. Solitaire slipped an arm under Gayle's back, pulling her around to face him. His hand spread on her aching lower back. "This is all the heat I can apply."

She stiffened, tried to pull away, but the radiant warmth of human touch felt so damn good, and in another few moments it felt so good that she didn't care that she was cradled in Solitaire's arms, her face inhaling her own hot dizzying breath against the shelter of his shoulder.

He was a cold, cruel man, Gayle reminded herself as she fell asleep, but nobody could complain about his body heat.

Solitaire felt sleep melt her body like sun-warmed toffee. Against the outside cold, he felt warm enough for two. Inside, a solid single lump of ice surrounded the hard brittle knot of his heart.

The woman in Cape Town had a name he never used and seldom thought. She had helped him, loved him. Died for him. He tried to let nothing touch him, but that had touched him. Now another woman, a strong-headed, stubborn, romantic woman with more guts than was good for her lay bruised in his arms, running for her life.

Rage hot enough to melt his inner ice burned low and constant deep inside him, perhaps where his soul should be. He wanted to stop it, *had* to stop it. Somehow.

He had hoped they would follow, the nameless killers

who always came. This time he would stop and stand and kill them if he could. The desert was his turf. It always had been. If only he had come to this one as he always had before: alone.

Gayle moaned in her sleep again, a soft, unnervingly sexual sound. He realized that his grip on her had tightened painfully and forced his fingers to relax, forced himself to forget the ugly dark blot on her body that was the price any woman who loved him was likely to pay. He had known better. Why had he done it, let her do it? To drive her away, too late? For nothing?

He remembered the morning fever that had tossed them together like driftwood caught in a current capable of mangling them both. He pulled her closer, into the furnace of his body and the ice of his emotions. His face brushed the soft texture of her hair. He inhaled a lingering scent of lemon shampoo. Such civilized signs would soon vanish into the stench of sweat and survival.

He brushed his mouth against her hair again, his simply sensing the silky strands, one by one. They lowered to her cheekbone, tickled by the invisible down delicate as mist on her skin. By the fevered heat of her cheek, he knew he caressed her injured side.

Gayle never woke or stirred. And Solitaire never shaped his lips into anything remotely resembling a kiss.

"Aargh!" Gayle groaned unglamourously, as she stretched forward to pull on one toppled boot.

"Don't move!" Solitaire's shadow loomed opaque against the dazzling daylight silhouetting him in the cabin doorway. He leaped toward her like a lithe black panther and wrested the boot from her hand.

"Never put anything on without checking for scorpions first."

He shook each boot upside down for a full minute, disgorging more sand than Gayle thought could insinuate itself into city boots, but no scorpions.

"Here, let me." Solitaire added, kneeling to help Gayle tug on the stiff leather.

His hands under her elbows boosted her upright without any strain on her back.

"How are you feeling?" he asked.

Gayle kept her eyes down, tucking in her shirttail as matter-of-factly as she could.

"You'll want to keep that shirt out." His voice knifed into her privacy. "Cooler."

She felt her color rise as she jerked the shirttail free again. "How am I feeling? Too soon to tell. I slept well."

He looked away, but the strain in his eyes told her that he had not. A memory of the warmth of his hand intruded, reviving the unasked-for desire she'd felt for him in the Crystal Phoenix casino.

She turned away so abruptly, her back rebelled with a punishing spasm. She ignored it.

"What a crazy . . . situation." Her voice sounded as if it shook from fatigue rather than confusion. "Where are we? What is this place?"

"Home sweet home."

Gayle looked up to see Solitaire leaning a proprietary arm against the rough red stone walls.

"The Brits say a man's home is his castle. Welcome to Castle Smith." He grinned self-mockingly.

"You've been here before."

"Many times. We're in that devil's workshop of iron-rusted sandstone called the Valley of Fire. They whisk tourists through on buses daily, but they never take them into the secret deeper crevices of the place. It's a huge area, shaped like a sitting fox, I've always fancied."

"But where is it?"

"A few miles west of Lake Mead."

"And what about your"—Gayle studied the circle of stones penning them in—"your summer palace?"

"Come out, but put on your hat and sunglasses."

Outside, a cobalt shield of sky curved over the earth. A ridge of umber cliffs rose rampant against it. Beneath the cliffs huddled three tiny sandstone cabins in a row, each offering one doorless entryway and one shutterless window.

"Civilian Conservation Corps works built these 'cabins' in the thirties, during your Great Depression."

"People stayed here overnight?" she asked in disbelief, eyeing the savage cliff-face with her sunglasses still in hand.

"Why not? You did. Shelter's not to be sniffed at on the desert."

She tilted her head to stare at him, still unsure, but aware that he was easy to look at. At least a woman wouldn't get a crick in her neck looking into his eyes.

"You hungry?" he asked, restless under her stare.

She followed him to the crumbling low rock wall where he'd set out their morning meal. Dehydrated eggs and sausage in a small frying pan sizzled over a mesquite-wood fire. A chunk of bread on tinfoil warmed in the sun.

Solitaire crouched beside his impromptu heath, pushing back the brimmed khaki hat that had materialized from inside his Santa Claus backpack.

"Eggs and sausage, really?"

"Amazing what they make for the nature lover these days."

She watched him flip sausage rounds with a fork. A

114

sudden vision of Joe at the big, six-burner stove overlay Solitaire's form, wavering in the early-morning desert heat like a mirage. Or was Gayle wavering, wavering on her feet? Or was it her eyes, were her eyes trying to stare through imperfect wavy glass, through tears?

"What's the matter?" Solitaire's face, turned over his shoulder, was mostly obscured by the hat brim. "Lost your appetite? Your voice?" He turned enough to see her eyes, his expression flattening.

"I . . . like men who can cook, that's all."

Solitaire had already turned away. "I can't afford your 'likes'. They're too lethal."

The rebuff thickened the tears in her eyes, but threw her a safety line of an anger as sudden and overwhelming as her sadness. She slapped the sunglasses into place on her face.

"Talk about 'lethal'! You've half killed me, dragging me out to who-knows-where, running from figments of your imagination, for all I know."

"That bruise isn't a figment."

"No. It isn't." She moved to the other side of the fire, searching for desert insects as he had warned her. "How long do we have to stay out here?"

"Until they find us. Or they don't find us." The hat brim, despite being snapped up on one side in tried-and-true Aussie fashion, draped his face in shadow. His tone was equally unrevealing.

"What does that mean?"

"It means that if they find us, they either kill us or we kill them."

" 'We'?"

He reached into the daypack to pull out a pistol. "Yours. Ever shot a pistol?"

"Only cap, and water."

He blinked, uncomprehending.

"You know, children use 'em?" She aimed a mock-lethal forefinger at the distance. "Bang, bang, you're dead."

"Well, this one means it. I'll teach you how to use it."

"And if they don't find us?"

"Then we gamble. I'll get you to an airport other than Las Vegas's and on the way home to Kansas, and hope they don't pick up your trail."

"And you?"

"I'll 'disappear' again, perhaps go to Canada, perhaps ship out to the Fiji Islands. Who knows?" He looked up, eyes intent. "Certainly you won't. Safer that way."

"Unless they find me and don't believe me."

He let the fork clang into the pan, then handed her a tin plate of a homogenized yellow-and-brown conglomeration. No wonder the military called meals messes, Gayle mused as she toyed with her food.

"That's why I'd rather they found us, and we kill them," he went on cold-bloodedly. "And it is 'we,' Gayle, because either you help me, or at least don't hinder me, or you help kill me."

Gayle stared at her scrambled eggs in the warming morning sun, growing cold. "You make killing sound so easy. Have you done it before?"

"No. I've run. Sometimes you get tired of running. Or you run right into something—or someone—that makes you angry at anyone who makes you run anymore. Sometimes a crowd is the most efficient form of solitary confinement. Eat your bloody eggs," he suggested tonelessly.

Gayle eyed her unappetizing plate, glancing up with sly eyes. "Actually, they *could* use some ketchup."

He leaned away to dig in the backpack, finally pulling out a foil packet and tossing it into her lap. Gayle tore it open with her teeth and squeezed out a carmine glob of Heinz.

"You must camp out a lot," she commented, downing the now truly bloody eggs.

"I like the solitude." He answered ironically, shoveling food mechanically into his mouth.

"Maybe you've gotten so used to doing what you *have* to do rather than what you *want* to do over the years that you don't know the difference anymore. I bet that if sand contained nutrition, you'd down it for breakfast every day."

She returned to contemplating her rubbery meal and her equally tough situation, but he spoke again, as if to fill the sudden silence.

"I was reared in a desert, right in the middle of Australia. They call it the Dead Centre. Or sometimes the Red Centre. It looked a little like this one—big and barren and incredibly beautiful."

The last word surprised her. She turned to survey the landscape, not having noticed beauty in it and not expecting Solitaire to succumb to beauty in anything.

"There's a subtlety to it," he went on. "Most people think the desert is plain, commonplace, dull. But six or seven hundred types of cactus thrive in this part of the Mojave alone. Millions of creatures live here, quite well. I had to shake the snakes and scorpions from the firewood I gathered last night."

Gayle stopped chewing, appalled to realize how dangerous it had been to collect firewood in the dark. Solitaire talked on without noting her reaction, as the solitary often do.

"Did you notice that almost-oversweet fragrance last night when we arrived?" Gayle shook her head. "See that low green-leafed plant all over the slope? Dune primrose.

The flowers open at night and make the desert into a perfumery."

"You know a lot about the desert."

"One could spend one's life studying it and barely encompass more than a grain of its sand compared to what remains to know."

"But you've lived other places, done other things. You talk about 'shipping out' so casually. You were at sea once?"

He laughed, harshly. "I'm always 'at sea,' clever Gayle." He bent to retrieve the eating utensils and etched a line between them in the rough sand. "I believe you're trying to do what nice young ladies are taught to do—'draw me out.' I don't 'draw out.' If you want to know something, ask me."

She added her empty plate and her fork to his pile before she spoke. "Maybe I want to know too much."

"I'll tell you if you do. Wager on it."

"Well, then." Gayle sat primly on her rocky seat, her booted feet together, and pushed Jill's Western hat back, though with the sunglasses he couldn't see her eyes. "Tell me all about yourself, Mr. Smith."

He shrugged, but his green eyes gleamed. Gayle laced her fingers together over her knees and tilted her head, a politely attentive expression turning her face into a parody of itself.

"Not much to tell. I left Australia when my problem . . . became obvious. Shipped to Java. Hit Hong Kong. Singapore. Cape Town you know about. Brussels. Now there's an out-of-character destination. Like to know more about it?"

"Not really. I don't care for brussels sprouts, anyway. So you went to large cities, to get lost in?"

He nodded. "Always work to be had in great metropolises, for not-so-great pay with few questions asked." He spread his oil-smudged hands, palms up, and regarded them with detached amusement. "If only the soft-palmed millionaires I refereed at the Crystal Phoenix had seen where these hands had been, what they'd done."

"They're smooth enough," Gayle objected without thinking, flushing when he glanced quickly to her face. His bottle-green glance cut her like broken glass.

"*Now*," he conceded. "But I've had my share of calluses and cuts and dirty fingernails. None of that would do at the Crystal Phoenix, but it's business as usual for hands that work at hauling cable, loading ships, chopping sushi, smuggling . . ."

"Smuggling?"

He looked up, wary again. Gayle realized he'd forgotten her for a moment.

"I helped smuggle boat people out of Cambodia for a while. Some international do-gooders recruited whoever would help."

"It must have been dangerous."

"I was probably safer on the south China seas than I was in Las Vegas. Poor bastards—all they wanted was *out*, and if the regime behind them weren't bad enough, there were schools of pirates who believed in free enterprise, waiting to pounce on them ahead."

"They were sitting ducks, I guess."

Solitaire stood suddenly. "We've got to get packed and moving. Tourist buses will be coming."

"It must have been hard," Gayle said gravely.

"What?"

"Keeping to yourself among all those desperate boat people clinging together."

"We didn't speak the same language."

Gayle pressed her lips together, then looked at him as directly as she could. "Solitaire, when did it happen?"

"What?"

"The first time."

"Are you prying into my sex life again?"

"The only 'first time' that really counts with you. The first time someone tried to kill you."

His shoulders dropped, but he kept his gaze on the distant, burning blue horizon.

"It was on a day much like this, in a place much like this. The Red Centre. The Dead Centre. I grew up on my uncle's water station. I was off by myself, and someone shot at me with a long-range rifle, that's all.

"I thought it was a fluke at first—no one much ever came out there anyway, for anything. But the shots followed me, and finally I was running for my life. I had just turned eighteen, and someone was taking potshots at me on my own ground. I ran, and I kept on running until they stopped shooting. Only they never did."

"And you've never known why?"

"Maybe it doesn't matter anymore."

"It does to me."

"Hell it does!" He turned, his mahogany face white at eyes and mouth. "It's facts, that's all. Statistics. It doesn't matter any more to you than it matters to me when you divorced your husband or who divorced whom or why! It's history. Who cares?"

Gayle looked from his angry eyes to the same horizon he found so consolable. "I guess you don't. But I've never been divorced."

A harsh rustle indicated Solitaire's disbelief, but Gayle ignored him.

"You said you weren't married anymore," he accused. "You must be divorced."

"I'm a widow. My husband died. So I'm *not* married any-more. But I'm not divorced. And you're right. It's history. Nobody should really care anymore about the fine points. But I do. People in Kansas are funny that way."

Gayle went back to the cabin to retrieve the sleeping bag. She had shocked him, she knew, and she wasn't sure why.

♠ ♠ ♠

They lunched under a prow of red wind-and-water-carved rock shaped like a huge tortoise. Gayle munched trail mix and cold roast beef. She studied an endless up-heaval of rust-colored stone reaching in every direction, raw nature untouched by humanity except for the ludi-crous toy Jeep painted powder blue that rested on a nearby rise.

"No one could find us out here," she declared. "We must be safe."

Solitaire, lying on his hip in the shade with the old map spread beside him, doffed the hat and ruffled his hair.

"Where there are maps, there are ways to find people. If those two can't do it themselves, they'll hire someone who can."

"Three? You expect *three* killers to follow us?"

"I don't expect their guide to be a killer, but once with them, I must assume he'll function as one, yes. Three."

"It's one thing for you to act like you're Mr. Solo, but you can't really believe you're James Bond? You can't outrun, outwit, outlast three men!"

"That's why we'd better take time for shooting instruc-tion." His expression grew wry. "Look at it this way. I've got an extra hand now too."

"Oh, damn! I'm no help to you, and you know it. You'll just waste bullets trying to teach me how to shoot."

"I don't have to teach you how to hit anything, just how to handle a gun."

"What's the good in that?"

"It's useful in close encounters. If I'm not there."

Gayle dusted her hands on her designer jeans. "If you're not there, it won't be much use for me to shoot anyone. I can't drive a stick shift. I can't tell a scorpion from a piece of sun-baked limestone. I can't find water, and I can barely walk in these damn boots!"

Without answering, Solitaire reached into one of his oversize pants pockets. A pair of glitter-dusted anklets arced toward her.

"Dry your feet in the sun and change socks. It makes a difference."

Gayle did as he said, scooting forward until her bare feet protruded from the shade to soak up the midday sunshine. Her reddened feet welcome fresh socks, punk or not, and Gayle found her back mended enough that she could pull on her own boots without grunting.

Solitaire didn't notice her achievement. He lay poring over the vintage map. How on earth, she wondered, had she ever considered such an uncommunicative man attractive?

A rock scraped behind her, startling her thoughts away.

Solitaire Smith suddenly loomed over her like a sandstone-carved statue, the strong light rusting his dark brown hair and turning his tan tobacco-colored.

"Ready?"

"Yes!" She jumped up to prove herself an intrepid outdoorswoman. The abrupt motion painfully reminded her of something she'd been trying to forget for hours. "Uh . . . no."

"No? What's wrong?"

Gayle glanced to the Jeep, imagining jolting over saw-toothed ridges for the next three hours.

"I really should . . . I have to—" She stuck her hands in her front jean pockets, even though they were so tight there was hardly room, and stomped nervously from foot to foot. "How do I—?"

"You haven't gone to the bathroom since we left Vegas?" He sounded incredulous again.

"Not exactly."

"You mean—you don't exactly mean that?"

"I mean I haven't exactly . . . gone."

The astonishment on his usually stoic face was far more shocking than having to ask him how to do such a basic thing in the desert.

"I don't know how!" she exploded. "Why on earth should I? And you told me to watch out for scorpions and foot-long centipedes and kiss bugs and diamondback rattlers and black widow spiders and, and—lions and tigers and bears, for all I know! It doesn't exactly encourage one to . . . relax."

He laughed. Solitaire Smith laughed. Gayle was so flabbergasted she forgot to notice what kind of laugh it was.

"You've got a first-class stiff upper lip, I'll grant you that. Come on, I'll take you behind the nearest rock and teach you the facts of desert life. Then we concentrate on the next most important thing. The gun."

♠ Chapter Nine ♠

Red all around had deepened into scarlet and wine. The rocks burned flame-bright, glaring back at the sunset-crimsoned clouds.

At Gayle and Solitaire's campfire-paired boot-toes, mesquite wood burned slow and bright, necklaces of twisting tangerine flame wreathing the spare branches.

Gayle watched the flames, mesmerized, feeling them flicker over her face and feet, feeling them dance in the tiny mirrors of her dreaming eyes.

"I don't want to die," she said. The pronouncement came in the wondering tones of a revelation.

"Maybe you won't," Solitaire answered prosaically.

Gayle clasped her hands around her knees and tried to read Solitaire's unreadable face by firelight. The licking flames seemed to play phantom expressions over it.

"Is that the best you can do, Mr. Bond?"

"It's the best anybody gets, a maybe. I simply happened to draw much longer odds." The firelight sketched a meager smile onto his lips. "Maybe I'm lucky, after all. Think how many men who've been hunted for twelve years are still alive . . ."

"You're not lucky for women," she noted carelessly.

Pain like red-hot lightning seared his features—or perhaps it was only a mask of it the firelight had painted on.

"I told you to stay away." He spoke between his teeth, like someone rebuffing a beggar. "I did everything I could to make you leave me alone."

"Yes, you did," she consoled him. "And it worked. I was

124

leaving. You would have been left alone again."

"Too late. It's always too late."

"Or maybe you give up too soon." His stony silence contradicted her. "Solitaire, you're thirty years old; you can't go on running and hiding forever."

"All that comment proves, Miss Bank Manager, is that you've got a good head for figures. Why can't you let me be? Why do you care how old I am? I do my best to forget it."

"I don't imagine you've had many birthday parties in your life," she answered mildly.

His laughter came in a short, bitter bark. "You've got a penchant for understatement, Kansas. My uncle and I ran the station alone. He never held with birthday parties, not even when I was a nipper. He was an . . . odd, unlikable man. I was going to leave the station as soon as I turned eighteen and he couldn't have me hauled back to work my tail off for him anymore. That's the only birthday I gave a tinker's damn about."

A stick from the dark stirred the snapping flames before he spoke again. "So someone with a rifle came along and gave me extra motivation to move on. Perhaps someone did me a favor. I've seen a lot of the world."

"What was her . . . name?"

"Her?" The darkness across from Gayle stiffened. "Who?"

"I'm the one who's supposed to play innocent, remember?"

"I don't want to tell you."

"Did you care for her?"

"Maybe . . . I could have. I never stayed long enough in one place to find out—with anyone."

"That's awful."

His face turned to her, his eyes glittering in the heated

light that moved and dappled like scarlet water.

"No, it isn't. Open your eyes, Gayle. That's the way most people live, even ones who come equipped with so-called roots and do everything by the book society writes for them. They work the same job, sleep with the same man or woman all their lives . . . sometimes, raise their children and finally die and leave whatever bit's left over to whoever wants to take it most."

"If life's so futile and you've learned to live with it that way, why won't you tell me her name?"

"Because it's none of your damn business!" Feeling thrummed under his voice. Gayle could almost sense the common ground between them humming to telegraph its angry message: *Leave me alone. Stop.*

"You can't bury the dead until you can say their names out loud," Gayle said, more to herself and the fire than to him. "I learned that the hard way." She studied the last thin cutting edge of sunset over the distant purple ruffle of mountains as she fingered the silver locket at her collarbone. "My husband's name was Joe."

"It would be."

Gayle ignored the taunt from the darkness. She felt alone, but unlike Solitaire, she knew she was not.

"It's a Kansas-kind of name," she agreed. "He was a Kansas-kind of guy. Decent, I guess you'd say. He believed in everything he was supposed to—himself, me, his work. The country. Kansas corn, right off the cob. He was good-looking, too—not showy, but just plain nice to look at. Or maybe he was just plain nice, and that's why you liked looking at him. He was . . . twenty-nine. When he died."

"Shut up." Pent-up emotion jarred the words free of their rudeness.

126

Gayle waited. In silence. The fire snapped from time to time. She huddled cozily into the lambskin jacket. She'd had a decent dinner, thanks to Solitaire's camping skills, had been to the bathroom before it got dark and had not encountered anything on two, four, six, or eight legs—or even worse . . . none. What more could a woman want? The night was pleasant and the tin cup of hot tea warmed her hands against the inevitably encroaching night chill.

"How"—the word came cautiously from the solitary dark—"How did he . . . die?"

Gayle smiled sadly into the flames, more at Solitaire's capitulation than at her memories. But she could smile at memories now, as well. She'd learned how to do that the hard way too.

"It was a . . . fire. Joe was a fireman. He'd saved some people, an old lady and a young boy, but he went back in. For a cat. He found it, too, in all that smoke, but he never came out. They gave me a posthumous medal, and they gave him a fine funeral . . . and they gave the little boy a new cat."

A tin cup slammed into the fire's center, spraying droplets of tea. The flames hissed like a snake. Hands from the night jerked Gayle to her feet to confront something so dark that not even the firelight could reach it.

"How could you do it?" He shook her savagely. "How could you do it to Joe and to . . . to Kansas and old ladies and little boys and bloody heroes and dead cats everywhere? To come from that and to come here and throw yourself at me? To end up out here, like this? How could you do that to him, to them, to yourself? To me?"

"I thought . . . I thought I could love you."

"Love?" He shook her again, but Gayle had retreated to an inner emotional landscape, and not even Solitaire could touch her there. "You've . . . affronted love! You've betrayed it. I don't know much about it, but I know I can't love, and if you can, you've got no right to throw it away, to waste it like that!"

"Love doesn't ask permission."

"Love's a delusion! If you want to follow it, fine. But leave me out of it."

"I already have. I said I thought I loved you. Past tense."

His fingers were loosening, one by one. "I see. You were . . . reminiscing just now. Burying your dead, me along with them, I hope."

Gayle hesitated. "You've always been left out of it. It's all been my initiative. I'm sorry I chased you. I couldn't seem to help myself. But I'm not sorry I've . . . known you."

"No one knows me."

"I think I'm beginning to."

His bitter laugh rang against the rocks again. "Still chasing delusions? That's hard to do, in the dark."

"It's easier, in the dark. Speaking of which, do you have the flashlight? It's getting cold and I want to find the tent."

Light clicked on, the beam full on her face. How did he do that, Gayle wondered, how did he know exactly where she was when she herself felt so lost in this utter, desert darkness?

She squinted her eyes against the direct glare and waited. She waited many moments while he held her under unwavering, bright scrutiny. Solitaire could be harsh when he felt threatened. Finally the beam swung to the ground at her feet.

"Follow the yellow brick road, Kansas. You'll get to Oz yet."

The flashlight beam paced her up the rough incline to the small canvas tent she'd help Solitaire pitch on high ground before dinner. It was hard to imagine them and the sleeping bag all fitting inside.

At the opening his hand touched her shoulder. "We'll put the jacket over the bag."

She let him help her out of it as night air in the low forties swiftly curled its icy fingers around her torso to take the jacket's place. Shivering with sudden cold, Gayle dropped to her knees and crawled into the low tent to burrow into the unzipped sleeping bag.

She waited for Solitaire to eel in after her and draw the zipper up. The bag didn't warm immediately, but Gayle sighed in expectation of that happy condition as she felt the sleeping bag stretch to another's dimensions.

She lay on her back, staring at nothing. It was scarier to actually lie on the desert floor, protected by no more than stretched canvas . . . and Solitaire, of course, which was a great deal.

He had a smell, she had learned; so did she. Everyone did who encountered circumstances stark enough to make it more readily discernable. Solitaire smelled like the desert: rich, mysterious, and slightly alkaline.

She couldn't feel even the brush of his shirt, but she sensed him. The light draw of the sleeping bag across her body implied the bulk of his nearby form. If she listened hard, terribly hard, she could detect the whisper of his clothing as his breath eased in and out.

Gayle held her breath while she listened to his, her nails digging into her palms. Every pore in her body seemed alerted to his presence, though with Solitaire, presence was often the same thing as absence.

He hadn't been absent tonight, she thought, remembering his voice rubbing raw with emotion. She wished she could have seen his face, and then, pictured it: the intriguing eyes blazing with feeling instead of shuttered with restraint, his beautiful face—and it was beautiful, Gayle had decided, not just attractive or even handsome—mobile and reacting to her, his mouth unconscious of itself for once, moving in ways that she felt in the very navel of her soul.

A pain, that was the only way to describe it, a pain of longing struck under her left collarbone and streaked down her arm. A heart attack. She was having a literal heart attack and needed emergency assistance from the only man available and the only one utterly unwilling to give it.

Gayle's body twisted spontaneously, rejecting its sense of deprivation, moving by itself to seek some small pleasure somewhere . . . perhaps in a new position.

"What's the problem?"

Solitaire's voice spoke so close it seemed to originate within her ear. For a moment she feared he could read her thoughts through mere proximity.

"My, uh . . . back. It hurts. Again."

"I thought your back was better."

"It is, but this ground is so hard!" Gayle tossed again to prove her false complaint true. "It'll get better."

The sleeping bag rustled massively. He was turning to face her. Gayle's heart debated skipping a beat then chose a wildly opposite course and began pounding in triple-time. She froze on her back, looking up at the dark. He used his arms again, to lift her off the hard ground, to buffer her discomfort.

There was nothing more to it.

She lay still and aching as their common warmth mingled and strengthened, as she wafted on the rhythm of his roughened breathing, afraid to ruin it. Gayle bit her lip to keep from moaning. Inopportune moans seemed to be a failing of hers with Solitaire, she thought ruefully.

She felt herself growing sleepy despite herself. Her cradled comfort, she knew, hung from the bough of his discomfort. She tried to speak but found her voice had temporarily deserted her. She tried again.

"I'm not making you uncomfortable?" *Wrong, wrong, wrong.* She meant putting his arm to sleep, giving him a crick in the neck, not . . . anything else.

In the silence she could hear him mentally considering responses.

"Uncomfortable?" He finally answered her with another question. "A bit. But it's no problem."

Oh, yes, she thought, you self-made celibate! You can lie here all night and not move a muscle—and probably will just to prove you haven't lost control. Gayle smiled and shut her eyes, letting sleep, a more tractable lover, seduce her. She had a little secret something of her own to prove.

She hadn't lied tonight, when she'd told Solitaire that she had thought she had loved him and no longer did. She hadn't lied at all. Now, she *knew* she loved him.

Gayle woke alone, as she always did.

She checked her watch. Despite awaking earlier each day, she'd never been able to catch Solitaire sleeping, no matter how much she wanted to wake first, brace herself on an elbow and study his unconscious face in the soft, infant daylight.

She wondered if he ever did as much for her, but rejected it as a romantic notion alien to his cautious personality. She didn't want to change him, she reminded herself, just to free him.

Crawling out of the tent, Gayle took the gun from the daypack and headed for a stand of creosote bushes. Now that she knew how to use it, Solitaire insisted she take the weapon along on excursions of a private nature.

Gayle decided she was beginning to feel distinctly unpretty, wearing the same clothing day after day, washing her hands and face with foil-wrapped towelettes, feeling her hair grow dull and flat. She felt in her jean pocket for the lump of the mirrored fabric case that held her lipstick and applied it. Then she peeked at herself. Hardly inspiring. Gayle sighed and put away the lipstick. She'd only eat most of it off again over breakfast anyway.

She made her way out of the scrub, the revolver aimed at the ground, proud of having survived another brush with necessity. It wasn't the lack of private toilet facilities that unnerved her, but the need to put herself in a distinctly vulnerable position with so many unseen desert perils abounding.

Solitaire had scrupulously cautioned her to avoid all forms of desert insect life, including so-called "velvet ants" whose sting, he said, felt like anything but. Gayle never shook out her boots in the morning without a hopefully unnecessary shudder.

"What's for breakfast?" she asked as she came up on Solitaire's campfire.

"Scorpions," he replied, as if reading her mind.

"Don't joke," she pled. Then stopped, standing above him. Solitaire never joked. "Or, if you must, pick a more palatable topic," she added lightly.

He glanced up at her, not quite smiling, not quite . . . not smiling. If he noticed the lipstick, he gave no sign.

"Buttermilk flapjacks," he said, flipping the silver-dollar-size circles in the black fry-pan bottom.

"Flapjacks? Oh, I love 'em!" Gayle got to her knees. "That's wonderful. But what'll we do when all this trail food you packed runs out?"

"The desert is the world's biggest delicatessen. We'll eat off the land, if we have to, but I hope that we won't."

"Eat . . . ?" Gayle gazed across the unproductive sand, studded with spare cactus plants and the cryptic tracks of uncounted nocturnal creatures. "What on earth—?"

"Everything on earth. Many of those inhospitable-looking cactus are edible. Some of them are botanical water-coolers, so to speak. There's more water out there than you'd guess, if one knows where to look for it."

"What about protein?" Gayle asked skeptically. "Man does not live by cactus spine and water alone."

Solitaire shrugged and flipped the flapjacks onto their plates. "Chuckwalla lizards—you know, those rock-colored blighters I showed you from the Jeep?" Gayle nodded like a dutiful student. "Well, they're fairly tame and they taste exactly like chicken."

"Chicken! *Arghh!* And what are these . . . black lumps in my flapjacks?" she asked suspiciously.

"You wanted protein."

"What are they?"

"Raisins. Quick energy. Quite, quite . . . dead. I shot them before breakfast."

Gayle sat back, laughing and attacking the first miniature pancake. "Serve you right if someone stirred an ant or two into your batter someday."

He glanced sardonically to her quickly emptying plate. "That's why I always let my taster eat first."

Her fork paused at her lips as she eyed the raisin-studded flapjack again. "You wouldn't just sit there and let me eat something disgusting," she asserted confidently, biting down. "*Hmmmm,* delicious."

"Sure of yourself, aren't you?"

His eyes were smiling at her, and so were his lips. He looked like a different man. Gayle couldn't find the urbane baccarat referee in the red velvet jacket in her mind's eye anymore. If she glimpsed him again, from a foggy distance, she would wonder why she'd ever been crazy enough to imagine herself attracted to him.

"Sure of myself? Not usually," she answered him honestly. "Usually, I'm not sure of anything."

His expression slowly sobered, so elusively Gayle couldn't say when it had happened. He looked as if he had remembered something he desperately wanted to forget.

Solitaire started eating his food, enforcing silence. Gayle watched him, stricken into respecting it.

He glanced away from her to the distance. To the rock-jagged horizon. He entered instant solitude, that mental escape-hatch he always kept accessible. The night swept out from the broom closet of her memory, the precious, tormenting night.

Des-per-ah-do . . .

This morning she had swept color onto her mouth to spotlight her smile, to shape it into a brave banner in the face of the monotonous wilderness.

Last night she said she had once thought she'd loved him, but no longer did. Last night she'd lain quiescent in his arms, accepting his obvious need and his right to deny it to both himself—and her.

This morning she prattled of pancakes and painted sunsets on her mouth. He couldn't encourage her, he told himself again. That would be the greatest cruelty. He might be dead in a few days. So might she, the hard voice that shared his mind needled. Another, slyer voice answered. Why not take what you can? You'll be gone anyway, one way or another. And so will she.

Solitaire reached for Gayle's empty plate and cup, his eyes avoiding the stubborn questing of hers. Brown eyes seemed born of honesty. He kept his on the changeless blue horizon.

He sand-washed the plates and packed them.

"We'd better get going." He stood.

"Solitaire, we *are* going . . . somewhere, aren't we? I mean, we're not just wandering around?"

His breakfast had left a bitter aftertaste, a fault of the dried flapjack mix or his own taste buds. He glanced at her face for a stolen second. Her eyes were the soft, meltable brown of milk chocolate, but only tropical chocolate with its higher melting point could survive in a desert, even an emotional one.

"We're not," he assured her without really saying anything, "just wandering around. Let's pack the Jeep and get going."

Her eyes hardened into the color of old pain at his curtness.

Solitaire tried to ignore the cold voice in his head adding "cad" into his long list of personal failings. He'd held her by his choice; he could . . . had to . . . let her go by his decision. They'd be coming soon, if they were any good at all. He had to be ready for them. In an equation that brutally life-and-death bare, Gayle Tyson was extraneous.

"How far can we go on that?"

Gayle watched Solitaire carefully pour the contents of the big, red five-gallon gasoline can into the Jeep's fuel-dry tank.

The mid-morning sun had warmed the air to just-this-side of hot, and Solitaire had stopped to take the ragtop down as well as refuel.

"Far enough," he answered in his old, close-mouthed way.

They had parked atop a ridge at the western edge of the Valley of Fire. When he climbed back into the Jeep, he pulled a pair of binoculars from the daypack in the back seat and scanned the horizon in a slow circle.

"We're leaving the Valley of Fire?" Gayle guessed. "Is that why you filled the canteens at that water hole? What'll we do for gas when we run out of this?"

"Find some. Like we did water." He listened as the engine started with a wheeze that grew into a gas-gobbling rumble.

" 'We' don't find anything," Gayle said. "You do."

"Better put your hat back on," he suggested, not looking at her as he babied the ignition. "The sun must be making you testy."

"No. It's just that . . . you don't need me, so there's no reason for you to pretend I'm anything other than a rather tiresome . . . impediment."

"Rather fancy word for it. Can't you be a simple burden like the rest of ordinary humanity?"

"I guess I've got a weakness for putting fancy words on basically shoddy realities," Gayle stung back.

"That's me, your basically shoddy reality," Solitaire answered her jibe, shrugging it off with the dry humor he'd begun exhibiting since they'd left Las Vegas.

Gayle's tears collected behind the extra-dark tint of her Solitaire-selected sunglasses. The Jeep jolted into gear and then plunged down the rough terrain, shaking rivulets of water onto her cheeks.

Gayle stared ahead, trying not to feel abandoned, betrayed, unvalued, and hoping that if she ignored the waterworks no one would notice. The tears wouldn't stop, bubbling up from a bottomless spring in her emotions. He had changed—again—back into the emotionless man whose passionate indifference had seared her very soul in a Las Vegas motel room only days before.

"Perhaps I oversell our . . . my ability to find water out here," Solitaire commented after a few minutes. "It's still a good idea to preserve what water we have; all forms of water." He had never even glanced at her wet cheeks, but he knew the tears were there.

She wanted to burst into a full-throated bawl. She wanted to crawl into a hidey-hole with a scorpion. She wanted to hit him—hard.

Instead she tightened her grasp on the Jeep's grip bar and held her breath for a count of twenty. It helped. The tears, found out, evaporated in the spreading, heedless desert Gayle cultivated over her inner landscape.

He didn't care; why should she? She didn't care if the killers found him—and her—and then nobody else ever found them again. They could die out here and dry up and drift away, forever together and apart, and call it poetic justice.

She politely refused his offers of between-meal cheese or trail mix, and even rest stops. She sat like one of the Seven Sisters, the wind-carved landmark stones in the Valley of Fire, and listened to the wind whistle dully in her ears.

Solitaire drove, perversely grateful for her silence. He knew he was redirecting his anger for his own weakness last night at Gayle's strength today, but she couldn't be allowed to cherish wrong-headed illusions. If he was exceptionally lucky, perhaps she would end up hating him.

When not watching the rough road ahead, he eyed the gas gauge. It'd been months since he'd driven this way, and the cache might not be there—or might be empty. He was counting on that cache.

Once they left the flame-bright phenomenon of the Valley of Fire, the desert flattened into its usual bland beauty, an after-dinner dessert of vanilla sand and mint-green scrub.

It rippled mile after mile to the feet of surrounding, distance-hazed mountain ranges. "Purple mountain majesty," Solitaire summed up to himself. Like many world travelers, he saw each land's clichés with the same fresh eyes that had coined the now-tired phrases a century or two before.

Finding the right place on the desert took a knack. Wind and sudden gully-washer rainstorms could shift landmarks into unrecognizable forms. Solitaire peered ahead, truly forgetting Gayle's presence beside him for the first time in a long, bumpy day of driving.

The gas gauge needle kissed the *E* and retreated coyly. On the next bump, it dipped below the empty sign. Only a few more miles of go left. Solitaire stopped the Jeep and stood upright, scanning the desert floor. He wiped his face with the bandanna from his neck. His sweat sprung as much from sudden anxiety as late-day heat.

"What's wrong?"

Gayle's voice sounded dry, unused. He waited to respond, hating the fact that he had no answer. And then he spotted a dull flash of silver about six miles away.

Solitaire hurled himself down into his seat and wrenched the idling Jeep into forward gear. "Nothing's wrong. We'll be there in no time."

Gayle stared into the undifferentiated emptiness facing them. She knew they drove north because the sun had hung on their left since noon and even now faded before taking its nightly dip into the milky clouds pooling in the west. Thoughts of the previous evening's spectacular sunset and the night that followed it left her cold and ashy inside, like a burned-out house. Solitaire had said it first: what a difference a day makes.

He drove purposefully toward a clump of palo verde trees, the delicate, green-barked desert hallmarks that reminded Gayle of tall asparagus stands back home. In Kansas. Green and gold, wind-blown Kansas . . .

Solitaire angled the Jeep to a stop and jumped out without waiting for Gayle. She saw why a second later. A decrepit shed sheltered among the palo verdes, a wooden shed so gray and weathered it merged with the landscape, like a chuckwalla with the ground. Solitaire turned and hailed her, relief infusing his voice with energy. "Come on! No one's here and you're safer with me."

"Then I'll stay here," Gayle started to say, stubbornly folding her arms.

The defiant sentence died half-unsaid. Behind Solitaire, still impatiently beckoning her forward, a figure materialized against the lean-to's black emptiness. Gayle stood in the Jeep, her mouth wide in unsaid warning.

"Wrong, my lad," the newcomer said. "I'm here! What luck we cross paths again, Sylvester."

It would be hard to say whose mouth dropped lower, Solitaire's as he turned to face an unexpected fellow traveler, or Gayle's as she heard Solitaire hailed by the name of Sylvester. She got out of the Jeep and slowly walked toward the shed.

"Wild Blue!" Solitaire was surprised enough to allow himself to sound astounded. "Hello, old chap." He shook hands with the wizened little man who stepped from shadow into the ebbing sunlight. "I wasn't expecting you to be about."

"You know me. I'm like you. I come and I go. This time I'm staying. I came out to check the cache and it's too late to get back to Glory Hole, 'less you can see in the dark like a puma, or Jilly. Who's your co-pilot?"

Solitaire turned to find Gayle standing behind him.

"Gayle Tyson," she said before he could stop her, stepping forward to shake hands with the old man.

"Wild Blue Pike," the fellow introduced himself. He glanced at the taciturn man beside her. "Sometimes these Limeys are kinda slip-shod on the formalities."

"Limeys never forget formalities," Gayle answered with a smile. She jerked her head sideways. "But he's an Aussie."

"Oh, is that what the lad is? He's been kinda contradictory about it himself."

"Why are you called 'Wild Blue'?" Gayle couldn't help asking as she stared into his marble-bright eyes. "For your eyes?"

The old man savored his mystery. "Mebbe. Or mebbe I've got a sorrowful disposition like our friend here. Or mebbe I was quite a hell-raiser in my youth."

"He flies," Solitaire put in dryly. "In a Piper Cub. Up in the wild blue yonder over the bleedin' desert. Looking for . . . mirages."

"A plane? You have a plane?" Gayle glanced at Solitaire, her eyes abrim with hope.

"A two-seater," Solitaire answered quickly, reading and rejecting her burgeoning idea. "No, what I've come here for isn't wings." He turned back to the other man. "It's a bit of that aviation gas you've got tanked away below-deck, Wild Blue. We'll be down to running on chuckwalla spit in another mile or two."

"Gas, sure. I can siphon you off enough to fill your tank. But, say, Sylvester"—the sky-blue eyes squinted toward the powder-blue Jeep beyond the party—"ain't that Jilly's Jeep? I ain't seen her in a spell, but she was still driving that heap when I did. Trust that girl to keep her head even in the face of a windfall."

"Yes, it's Jill's Jeep."

"Didn't know you knew the half-pint. I figured you was jest some lonesome-lost desert rat like myself and the Glory Hole boys. Ever'time I run into you out here, you're alone."

"I know." Solitaire's level voice held an edge that made Gayle glance at him sharply. "But I know Jill from the city. I needed desert transportation in a hurry, so I . . . borrowed the Jeep."

"Jilly partin' with her Jeep? That's like tearing me from the sky, or pulling a kangaroo rat from a rattler's jaws. Say, did Jilly know you were . . . borrowing this Jeep of hers?"

Gayle put her hand through Solitaire's arm, presenting a united front to the forthcoming accusations of thievery, unfortunately justified. Solitaire didn't appear to notice or appreciate the gesture.

"Not . . . exactly," he answered. "I didn't have a chance to tell her."

Wild Blue Pike's eyes narrowed, then his age-cracked face heaved into a laugh. "On the lam, is it? You look a fellow who might know a little about adventure. Well, you come to the right place, boy. I'll give you your gas, and what's more, you and Miss . . . Tyson, is it? . . . can camp in the shed tonight.

"But"—the genial face tightened—"if you don't get that vehicle back to Jilly almost as good as new, me and the Glory Hole Gang will track you through every square foot of this waste and take it out of your mangy hide, Sylvester."

Wild Blue turned to Gayle. "Pardon the plain talk, ma'am, but there are certain laws of good conduct, even out on the Mojave."

Gayle let her arm drop, amazed. Sylvester . . . Solitaire led a charmed life. The old man was practically giving him the stolen Jeep and gas enough to run it.

"I'm glad to hear there are laws of good conduct even out here," she answered the old man with a smile, moving to take his spindly arm. She led him a few steps away and lowered her voice to her most confidential tone.

"Is it possible you have an extra sleeping bag with you? If you wouldn't mind, you and . . . Sylvester could share one and I could have the luxury of some solitude."

"Only one sleeping bag between you?" Wild Blue's spry voice crackled with loud indignation. "I've heard of the running-out-of-gas trick before, but this little shenanigan beats all. Well, Miss Gayle, I'll be happy to provide you with your own kit. I guess it goes to prove that boys will be boys, even out on the desert."

"Don't worry yourself over it, Mr. Pike," Gayle replied in silken tones. "I think Mr. Smith is aging rapidly."

"Wild Blue's the name, Miss Gayle," he corrected, pinching her elbow fraternally.

"Oh, please, just Gayle," she responded in kind.

They laughed the joint, easy laugh of new acquaintances with one key thing in common.

In the rapidly oncoming dusk, Solitaire Smith stood apart, flinty-eyed, watching them.

♠ Chapter Ten ♠

"Sure a shame you wouldn't bed down with Gayle and me in the shed."

Wild Blue arched his back until it cracked and picked his way over the rock-strewn ground to Solitaire's morning campfire. He threw the rolled sleeping bag on the ground.

"Got right chill last night."

"As shelter, your shed isn't worth the wood shavings it's built from," Solitaire returned. "It's shelter of the purely psychological sort, which Gayle could probably use right now." He offered the old man a steaming tin cup. "Besides, I was on watch."

"Oh?" Wild Blue squatted beside the younger man. "Expectin' someone?"

"Several someones," Solitaire admitted tersely. "Best you get on your way and I on mine. Perhaps"—he hesitated a bit too long for someone who so firmly knows his own mind— "perhaps you could take Gayle back with you."

"Nice-lookin' woman," Wild Blue mused as he stared into the morning-glory sky his nickname came from. "Lady-like, too. Real nice and ladylike. Does toss and turn at night, though; whimpers up a storm, moans like. Anything wrong with her?"

Solitaire's face became a stunned blank. "Wrong? Nothing that getting out of this desert and back to civilization won't cure. She's simply uneasy. Gayle's not used to outdoor life."

"*Hmmm.* Well, sure, I'd be happy to march her back to Glory Hole, but it's a long trot for a city girl. I leave the

Piper at the halfway strip on short hops. Me and Sairy Jane come out the rest of the way alone, you know."

"Where *is* your better half?"

Wild Blue stared at Solitaire. He'd never before heard his desert-met friend employ sarcasm or any other turn of phrase that implied a sense of humor.

A lugubrious bray from behind a large fuzzy-spined cactus announced a presence. Moments later, a gray muzzle, topped by long limp ears, poked into view.

"No, I don't suppose Gayle could ride Sairy Jane," Solitaire concluded after eyeing the elderly little donkey. "But she could probably make the walk back to the plane."

"Consider it settled." Wild Blue dipped his face to the steaming cup to take a first sip, then sputtered. "Jumpin' boiled shirtcollars!" The old man flung the liquid into the nearby brush. "This is that Limey grasshopper juice, not real honest-to-bean brewed coffee! No wonder you're such a close-mouthed fellow. Takin' this tea stuff regular could sour a man."

Solitaire laughed, another out-of-character reaction, and reached into his down vest.

"Chin up, mate. I think I've got a clue to your heart's desire. Can you read this old map?"

"Ain't a map drawn I can't read, if I can see it proper."

The old man squinted over the unpleated paper for some time, taking off his hat to smooth the thin silver strands of hair veiling his bald head.

"Old, all right. Yep, I see Mirage Springs on here—ain't hardly no one nowadays who knows where that is. And—" Wild Blue pulled the wrinkled paper close to his famous eyes and chewed his puckered bottom lip for some time.

"Where'd you get this, Sylvester?" he asked sharply.

"Borrowed it," came the spare answer.

"*Hmm.* Don't suppose you'd say where?"

Solitaire's dark head, as yet unsheltered from the early sun, shook discouragingly.

"You know about the lost, er, treasure, so to speak?"

"I read the papers, even if I can't brew that battery acid you call coffee," Solitaire answered, his chameleon-green eyes glittering. "I know that most of the Carson City silver dollars you and your Glory Hole mates heisted forty-five years ago are still buried out here somewhere. I figure someone must have mapped exactly where—once."

Wild Blue slapped his blue-jeaned knee. The whip-sharp sound set Sairy Jane's Walter Denton voice asawing.

"He mighta done it! That . . . snake in sheep's clothing! That spotted skunk, Jersey Joe Jackson, who run off years ago with the silver dollars Jilly found at the Crystal Phoenix Hotel a year or so back—"

"Whoa, there. I know Jill and Johnny Diamond found some silver dollars in the old hotel suite Jersey Joe lived in since the forties. I also know that if it weren't for the statute of limitations, you and Jill's grandfather and all the good old boys who hang out at Glory Hole would be facing prosecution for the original robbery. What I'm asking is, if Jersey Joe did bury the money and did make a map and this is it, what's the key to exactly where the money's buried?"

"Let me see that map!"

Solitaire pulled it from Wild Blue's over-eager grasp. "This is my treasure hunt, old man."

"It's my treasure!"

"And my life that's on the line. I told you, they're after me. I'm simply curious. Perhaps I can confirm the location of the cache, among other things, if I live to tell about it. Whoever's got the best claim can keep the money."

Wild Blue's face grew sullen, then wily, and finally conceding as Solitaire watched it closely.

"All right, Sylvester lad. You're jest too smart for the likes of me. I'll tell you what I been flyin' these indigo skies most of my life to find—the last camel. That's what I saw from the air when Jersey Joe was down on the ground scouting for a hiding place. If I could sight that last camel again, we'd have the loot!"

"Last camel? I'd heard you had some fixation. You don't actually mean—?"

"Aw, not a livin' camel, boy, like that poor moth-eaten old beast they keep corralled near the highway for the tourists to gawk at. A *stone* camel. A set of rocks sittin' by themselves that look like a one-hump dromedary, if you want to get technical."

Solitaire refolded the map. "Wind and water could have eroded your last camel into a porcupine over forty-five years, Wild Blue. Maybe they ought to call you Wild Goose."

"Call me what you want. I know it's out there. And I'll keep lookin'. Whether you laugh and whether you keep your map to yourself, I'll keep lookin'."

"You do that." Solitaire stood and threw the dregs of his cup onto the campfire. "In the meantime, get Gayle back to Glory Hole. And you take good care of her."

Wild Blue stared as Solitaire went to the Jeep, throwing the sleeping bag atop his already-packed gear, and mounted it.

"Hey, Sylvester," he called, "ain't you gonna say goodbye to Gayle?"

The Jeep's motor was choking into life on the new tankful of odd-octane aviation gas. But the engine caught. Solitaire backed up to take a running start at the morning. Ahead of him, the sun's Midas touch was turning the desert sands into a treasure trove of pure gold, not silver.

"Solitaire!"

Gayle, emerging from the shed with half-open eyes and fresh lipstick, saw only an expanding storm of sand and the Jeep churning in its eye.

She stamped a frustrated foot, creating her own mini-dust storm. "Solitaire Smith! Dammit!" She was running past a stunned Wild Blue toward the Jeep. "Don't you dare! Don't you dare leave me behind! Solitaire—!"

The sand cloud subsided, revealing the Jeep shrinking at its center. Deserted in the desert, Gayle stared speechlessly at Wild Blue Pike. Then she twisted to face the arid open spaces again. The powder-blue Jeep bounced along a sinuous pale snake of misbegotten road that doubled back on itself like a hairpin before straightening to pin the distance to the blue-gold horizon.

Gayle inhaled an unhappy gulp of morning air, tightened her grasp on the hat "borrowed" from Jill along with the rapidly disappearing Jeep, and began running through the low-growing scrub in her fuchsia designer boots.

She had little hope of crossing the neck of the hairpin curve before the Jeep finished circling, but she ran anyway, shouting into her own dust.

The smoother ground near Wild Blue's buried gas tank soon roughened into scrub-dotted ridges of sand. Ahead, desert growth that had looked as small as an architect's model trees from a distance loomed larger, taking the form of tall yuccas and palo verde trees. The landscape in-between was a sand-beige pincushion dotted with knee-high teddy-bear cholla cactus, whose fuzzy forms always struck Gayle as resembling silver-green many-legged tarantulas . . .

She shuddered and ran on, dodging chollas, sliding onto the sides of her feet and hearing the fine, dyed leather scrape itself raw on the gravelly soil. The Jeep was swinging around, moving Solitaire at a right angle to her. He couldn't claim he hadn't seen her now.

She stumbled and fell forward, the heels of her hands braking on gravel. Her feet kept moving and she stumbled back up into a run again. Crushed at her feet, nameless floral scents percolated like morning coffee, some sweet and thick, others sour or lightly medicinal.

The desert she heedlessly charged through unfolded in the full, dazzling bloom it offers every seven years. Solitaire had mentioned it was due for a flower show. Hundreds of white, yellow, purple and pink blossoms ambushed her eyes, each flower as richly surprising as ruby-ripe strawberries hidden among smudges of dull green leaves. Gayle ran, feeling the colors whirling around her, the scents smothering her, feeling her legs growing leaden. The tiny image of a Jeep bucked into the irretrievable distance.

She thought she shouted, but the pounding in her ears muffled every sound except the distant waspish buzz of the Jeep's engine. The instant the sound began to wane goaded her like a whip. She ran faster, unable to overleap the plants in her path. Her oafish boots kicked through an obstacle course of prickly teddy-bear cholla, their chubby spined arms breaking off like limbs from over-loved dolls. Pain blind-stitched her side, invisible but effective, like her thoughts.

He wasn't waiting for her. He wasn't stopping. He wasn't going to let her come with him anymore. The realization weighed as heavy as heartbreak. Gayle's boots pounded the desert floor, matching her ponderous, slow-motion heartbeat.

Solitaire was going off to die, without her, like Joe. Not because it was his job and she couldn't be there, but because it was his life, and he simply didn't want her in it.

I'm sorry, Gayle thought, knowing her once-chic boots trampled delicate petals, crushing them into a heady, almost soporific natural attar. *I'm sorry, but* . . . She kept running, so tired, but until she dropped, she would run—

A humming in her ears churned into a disembodied cascade of noise. The desert whipped itself into a horizon-wide dust devil and angrily buzzed toward her. Out of the heart of the tumult came the mechanical wind-machine monster to meet her—a powder-blue Jeep.

Disbelieving, Gayle slowed and stopped. The Jeep swooped in front of her, so close that Solitaire's extended brown hand easily clasped her forearm.

"Get in," he yelled, pulling as she jumped into the rear seat. She gratefully sank atop the lumpy backpacks.

Her teeth vibrated as the Jeep circled back to the rough trail. Gayle turned to wave her hat at Wild Blue, or at least in the direction she thought he should be. Already, the shed and the palo verde stand had vanished into the desert's overwhelming anonymity.

Gayle climbed into the front seat and risked an inventory of Solitaire's profile. It was a cliff-face of sheer Aztec sandstone, like the time-carved rocks of the Valley of Fire, its anger-ruddied planes taut with inner tension.

Gayle shivered in the strengthening sunlight, gasping for words that wouldn't come until her lungs worked more placidly.

"Get your comb," was Solitaire's curt greeting.

Mystified, Gayle turned to dig in the daypack, trying to remember where Solitaire had stashed it. This hardly seemed the time to bother with combing their hair. She finally produced the familiar length of tortoise-shell plastic and handed it to him.

His hand left the steering wheel to examine the teeth, then returned it.

"Comb the teddy-bear cholla off your pant legs and anywhere else you find them," he began in an instructive tone. "Cholla sap is virulent. It can cause a severe skin rash, like poison ivy." He paused while the wheel bucked under his white-knuckled grip. The Jeep had left the token trail and was jolting across even rougher country now.

"You were running through a whole—" Solitaire paused to delete an expletive that must have been strong enough to corrode steel, "field of them, like they were bloody poppies or something."

Gayle decided the deleted expletive must also have been alliterative. Meekly, she began currying her pant legs.

"Why," she asked finally, "did you leave me?"

He didn't answer, wouldn't answer. The silence lasted long enough for Gayle to curse herself for asking the question no woman ever gets honestly answered and that no man ever welcomes being asked.

"I watched last night," he finally said, perhaps initiating a safer topic. "I spotted another campfire with the binoculars."

"It could have been . . . just nature-lovers."

This time he didn't answer at all.

"Truce?" Gayle asked when they stopped for lunch. They sat in the open Jeep, munching trail mix and the tropical chocolate Solitaire had salted into the packs.

"If you'll answer one question."

"Sure." Gayle was amazed it was going to be so easy. "I'll answer anything."

"Why did you run after me like that? If you had stopped

to think, going back with Wild Blue was an ideal solution to our situation."

Gayle let a piece of the slow-melting chocolate dissolve on her tongue while she searched for an answer.

"Maybe I didn't think. Maybe that's it. And I don't believe that walking away from you is a 'solution to our situation.' It wasn't when I tried to leave Las Vegas."

"Did you give it a chance? Did you even try?" Solitaire swept the outback hat off his head to his knee, studying the distance through tobacco-dark sunglasses. "Gayle, do you ever do yourself the courtesy of thinking first? Or do you simply run after everything hell bent for leather, no matter what the cost?"

She leaned into the corner of the seat, seeking a defensive position.

"I—I'm a very cautious person."

He sighed explosively in contradiction.

"I am! That's all a woman can be, growing up in Canton, Kansas. I don't know why I'm acting so impetuously lately. Maybe I just feel that we're in this thing together."

"We are now," he agreed grimly. He twisted over the seat for a water canteen while Gayle cautiously measured his expression. It wasn't merely controlled anymore, or carefully tense, but deeply unhappy, she realized.

"I guess I've really screwed things up for you," she said.

His fingers froze on the canteen cap. "Are you speaking literally or figuratively?"

"Both, I guess. I should have known you'd go after what you wanted. If you wanted it. You know how to play the game better than anyone."

"Do I?" He frowned into the distance, as if alone.

"Solitaire? Are you listening? Your mind seems miles away. Do you . . . see something?"

He turned back to her. "Thousands of miles away, Gayle. You still don't see it. It isn't that I know what *I* want, it's that I don't want anything." He glanced away again. Through the sides of the sunglasses, Gayle could see his eyelashes blinking like confused semaphores.

"You don't want me," Gayle admitted quietly. "I know that."

"It's not you! It's anything that'll tie me down, slow me down, mess me up. Things, anything other than cold cash or gold coins, anything that isn't easily portable or convertible into another currency: people—friends or even so-called . . . would-be lovers. It has to be that way; it simply does."

"You must have known . . . some . . . women."

"Women!" He turned to her, wrenching off his sunglasses. His pupils retracted to pinpoints in the bright sunlight, turning his eyes into emerald-green target rings.

"Women pursue the unavailable man. You're not unique, Gayle. What drew you to me was my very disinterest. I've been with women before you. When I was young, I bought them, or they bought me, or we bought each other for free. It could have been the same at the Crystal Phoenix, but it wasn't. By the time Helene died three years ago in Cape Town, I had already decided he travels fastest who travels alone; he sleeps soundest who sleeps alone."

"Why do you always tell me only tawdry things about your past?" she demanded.

"Because it is . . . was tawdry. Only Kansas isn't tawdry nowadays. And you belong there. Without me. Here. Have some water."

The abrupt change of topic caught Gayle off-guard, with a thick lump in her throat that told her she felt like a fool.

"I'm not thirsty," she declined.

"Take water every chance you can in the desert." The canteen nudged her way again. "Drink."

She did finally, trying to swallow more than tepid water, maybe it was her pride. Screwing on the top again, thoughtfully, Gayle met Solitaire's always-vigilant eyes. "Why bother coming back for me just now, then?"

"You were blundering through Rash Heaven like a girl running through a field of daisies in a perfume commercial. Somebody had to set you straight. Besides, it's April Fool's Day."

"Oh. Maybe that's why I ran after you. And maybe you're blundering through Overcautious Hell and somebody needs to set you straight. But I think I got them all off."

He looked even more blank.

"The cholla spines. I suppose I better wash the comb before I use it again, though."

"Wash . . ." He stowed the canteen and started the Jeep. "Not a bad idea. If we get there before sunset."

"You're not talking about a real wash, like a bath?" Her skin shivered at the idea of clean water.

"Genuine wet water."

"In the desert? I know you say that water has a way of surprising one in the desert, but not enough to wash in."

"Enough to swim laps in," he answered a trifle smugly.

"That'd be nice," Gayle conceded, twisting a strand of dust-dulled hair between her fingers. "That would be absolute heaven . . . Sylvester."

She eyed him sideways. When there was no reaction, she was forced to seek one. "Why'd you tell Wild Blue your name was Sylvester?"

"Because it is. And I feel different on the desert than I do in Las Vegas. I told you Solitaire was show business."

"You are a different person here, in a way."

That drew his glance. Gayle smiled. "But not really. Wherever you are, the real you manages to play hide and seek."

"The real me." He shook his head. "You are a fatally presumptuous woman, Gayle."

" 'Fatally presumptuous'." I like that. If I'm going to be called names, I'd rather it be something . . . original. But I don't blame you," she added quickly. "You haven't seen the real me, either."

"What is the real you?"

Gayle leaned into the worn upholstery and contemplated the jolting horizon.

"The Real Me's never eaten anything more exotic than the stir-fried special at Denny's. The Real Me would never buy a blouse with white cuffs because they might get dirty. The Real Me can stand up for herself if she has to, but she'd prefer that people wouldn't make her—and they always do. She doesn't like to gamble, not even nickels, and she never picks up men. She can't do any one thing terrifically, but she can do an awful lot of things pretty well. And she's got a great imagination."

"So I noticed."

"But she doesn't know anything about what it'd be like to know people who wanted to see her dead, and she's never been outside the U.S.A., and she never dreamed that there were real women named Helene in real cities in a faraway, real world, who could die for knowing real men who might or might not be named Sylvester."

After a pause in which the Jeep bounced them over ridge and dip, he spoke without looking at her. "I let that slip, did I? The Real You doesn't miss much. It wasn't that melodramatic, Gayle. I found out about . . . Helene after, when I read the newspaper, and read between the lines. Of course I'm a living jinx—don't you think I know that? I'd simply like to keep my ill luck to myself. If people would let me," he added darkly.

Gayle watched Solitaire concentrate on nosing the Jeep over rugged terrain. A soulful melody ached at the back of her journey-worn mind.

Des-per-ah-do. . . .

Why couldn't he open the gate and see that he needed her?

Gayle looked to the mountains, which never grew closer no matter how long the Jeep ground toward their distant profiles. They were like Solitaire himself, she brooded, remote, tantalizing, aloof. Only the endless erosion of time could alter them: wind, water, or possibly the eruption of some dampened inner volcanic fire. Gayle guessed that the Real Her from Kansas didn't rank much above zero on the Richter scale of irresistible forces.

Solitaire wrenched the wheel. The Jeep plunged down an incline. They were barreling through shoulder-high stands of creosote bushes, the tires pummeling rocks and gravel.

"What is it?" Gayle twisted to scan the horizon for pursuers.

Solitaire's expression remained doggedly noncommittal, but after a few more spirals down the rocky path, Gayle completely forgot him for the first time in more than a week.

She half-stood in her bucking-bronco of a seat.

"It's . . . it's a tree! Out here in the middle of nothing! The widest, biggest tree I ever saw. Is it a . . . mirage?"

"In a manner of speaking."

She looked to Solitaire's face for confirmation of what she saw. His mouth twitched in a fashion that could only be described as an incipient smirk.

"Is it just growing there for the fun of it?"

"If you can call sitting in the same spot for four or five hundred years fun, I imagine you could say that."

Gayle bounced down into her seat and curled her fingers into his shirtsleeve, convulsively shaking the fabric.

"Solitaire, don't tease! Tell me where we're going."

He pointed to the tree waving its gold-tasseled top over the small ridges between it and them. "It's a salt cedar. Old as the foothills from its size. And it's growing there because it has a secret."

He hurtled the Jeep over one last sandy hummock and stopped it. Below them, in a cup of sere sand backed by an outcropping of reddish rocks, water rippled under the invisible teasing of the dry desert wind.

Gayle stood again, speechless.

"Mirage Springs," Solitaire said. "Just where the map said it would be. The answer to a Kansas maiden's prayer. Bathwater."

"It's safe to go in? Really?" Gayle didn't wait for an answer but jumped from the Jeep and bolted for the rush-edged pool.

The venerable salt-cedar tree, lush-limbed as a weeping willow but far sturdier, commanded one end of a pond perhaps 150 feet in diameter. At one side, a natural spillover tumbled down a ledge into a miniature waterfall, chuckling to itself.

"Watch where you're running," Solitaire was saying as he followed her, but his tone was tolerant, and his arms sagged with supplies from the Jeep. He tossed the daypack to the gritty desert floor, then turned to view the springs with hands on hips.

"You may be glad to see it now, but think how much

more it meant to foot travelers a century ago. Well, aren't you going in?"

"Can I?"

He squatted by the water's softly lapping rim to shake a hand in the sun-warmed liquid. "Feel it."

Gayle crouched beside him, trailing hesitant fingers in the muddy water. Tiny needles of nimble motion stitched a frantic zigzag pattern away from her hand. She jerked it back with a splash.

"Fish!"

"They've got to eat too." Solitaire smiled. "Maybe your hand's the best thing they've seen in a century. Try again."

She consulted his laughing eyes. In the shade of his hat brim, the green eyes that fascinated her had deepened to a mossy black. Smiling, watching him and not the water—because a laugh on Solitaire's face was as rare as a hidden spring in the desert—Gayle dribbled her fingers into the pool.

"What do you feel?" he was asking.

Gayle's eyes paced the perimeter of his face, snared by the hidden something she had always seen in it. Maybe it was a mirage, like the spring, she thought. Her fingers fluttered of their own volition. She glanced down to the water.

"Hey, it's *warm!* And not just because of the sun?"

"Not this early in the year," he confirmed. "Mother Nature herself personally heated your bath water."

"A hot spring! I've never seen one."

"Better stop looking and start splashing. Here, I'll get your boots off."

She sat and thrust out her feet while he wrenched off the sand-scarred boots, then she turned back to regard the water.

"Are you sure it's safe? It looks kind of murky—"

"That's because there isn't enough of it to reflect a piece of the sky."

"How deep is it?"

"Enough. You ask a lot of questions, Kansas. You're all questions and no action. Answer 'em yourself."

Solitaire pulled Gayle to her stocking feet and pushed her toward the water.

She resisted, screaming, her feet churning in the shallows, splashing his pant legs. He sent push fast behind shove. Gayle found herself backing away from him, knee-deep in tepid water while Solitaire watched housecat-dry from the shore.

"It . . . is warm." She bent to skein her hands through the gently stirring water. Her face reflected back at her through a surface as blurred as an ancient, wavy-glassed mirror. "It's wonderful."

She sat suddenly in the shallow water, wind-milling her arms and legs through its viscous layers. The late-afternoon sun baked her shoulders and the top of her head. She plastered a dripping hand to her still-dry hair.

"My hat! I mean . . . Jill's hat! Where is it?"

Solitaire laughed as she madly patted the water in a searching pattern.

"It's here!" He lifted it in his hand. "Take off your clothes, and I'll lay them on the creosote bushes to sun-dry."

Gayle stood in the knee-high water, dripping wet. "Take off my clothes?"

"Only the outer ones," he amended.

"Right." Gayle began unbuttoning her sopping shirt, glancing up from the awkward task now and then to gauge his reaction.

He was watching her from the shore, waiting and

watching, his head cocked so his hat brim protected his naked eyes from the four-o'clock sun slowly sinking over her shoulders. He wasn't leering, but he wasn't looking away either.

Undressing outside like this, in plain view, would have mortified the Real Her from Kansas.

But the Real Her from Kansas hadn't spent several adventure-packed days and nights wanting a stranger who refused to want her back. Gayle peeled off the shirt.

Stoic Solitaire watched poker-faced. But he watched.

"Throw it here," he said.

She did. By the time he'd straightened from plucking the shirt from the water's margin, she had her jeans unsnapped and unzipped. The wet denim had stiffened. She bent to pull first one foot and then the other free, then held out the water-logged mess.

"Toss," he said again.

This time she hurled the heavier jeans right into his hands.

Gayle stood unmoving, knowing she looked indecently white of skin for this rough-and-ready environment. She stood there in her J. C. Penney peach cotton bra and bikini brief set, watching Solitaire watch her.

"You're not getting very wet," he said finally.

The water rippled between them, separating them by perhaps thirty feet. It seemed like too much, and not enough.

His eyes lowered, slowly, by almost undetectable notches of his eyelashes. He turned—the bastard turned, Gayle raged to herself—and walked away.

"Monk!" her mind hissed at him in farewell. She churned into the deeper water at the center of the pool and sank up to her shoulders. It was like being submerged in

warm cream of mushroom soup. She could feel the water gently bubbling around her, or was that tiny fish lips!

An object arched out of the blue heavens. She caught it automatically.

"Lather up," Solitaire urged from the shore. Behind him, her empty clothes lay spread-eagled, straw-man fashion, on the creosote bushes.

It felt divine to slide the plain bar of soap over her dust-clogged pores. Gayle soaped herself twice, all over, and rinsed off. Then she waded to the tiny laughing waterfall, and sat on the rocky bottom stones while she dangled her legs into the plunging water. It massaged her like a tepid Jacuzzi.

Solitaire came overland to watch her.

"I'm getting fuzzy," she fussed, aware of cactus stubble on her unshaven white legs.

Wordlessly, he went to daypack, dug in it and returned to toss her a disposable razor. When she stared at him in amazement, he ran a hand over the three-day beard that smudged his lower face.

"I'll do better not shaving. It'll keep the sun—and wind-burn down. But you can."

Gayle shrugged and lathered her leg below the knee. "It makes you look like an escapee from *Miami Vice*. Some guys would kill to come by that look naturally."

"Not in Kansas."

"No."

"And watch your choice of verbs."

"Oh. Sorry."

Solitaire sat on a nearby rock, half playing lookout, half keeping an eye on Gayle. Self-conscious, she performed the shaving ritual with tried-and-true television commercial grace, pointing her toes and poising her legs ballerina-style.

160

It still didn't add any icing to what was essentially a bizarre, rather silly social convention. She was glad when she could toss the razor back to Solitaire.

"Aren't you coming in too?" she wondered.

"Later. One of us should be dry enough to play lookout. Why don't you scoot down to the lower level and use the falls like a shower jet, wash your hair?"

Gayle drew up her fish-white, semi-unclothed torso. "I don't 'scoot,' " she said haughtily.

Solitaire leaned forward, grabbed her elbows, and pulled her onto dry land and, for a moment, against him. Gayle dripped relentlessly onto his clothing, turning the khaki dark in great coin-sized blotches.

He quickly pushed her toward the bubbling waterfall. Gayle collapsed under the warm spurting water and soaped her hair, rinsing it until it squeaked for mercy. By the time she emerged, her eyes still squeezing half shut from the soap, Solitaire was waiting with a towel, a fresh pair of punk-rock socks, and her boots.

When her feet at least were "dressed," he jerked his head over his shoulder. She followed him curiously to the other side of the great salt cedar tree, where he'd spread the sleeping bag.

"Taking a sun bath will dry your clothes. There's the sunscreen. Use plenty. I've scouted for creepy crawlers and left you the pistol. Just in case."

His sun-browned hands reached toward her water-dewed cleavage. Gayle's heart leapt over the mountains. He patiently extracted the bar of soap from the hands she'd unconsciously clasped to her breastbone and turned away.

"Where are you going?" she demanded in sudden panic.

"My turn."

Watching him duck around the salt cedar branches,

Gayle settled on the closed sleeping bag. Its poplin surface was hardly satin, but at least it repelled water. While her body shed morose water drops onto it, she considered adding some salt water of her own.

Through the veiling branches of the spreading salt cedar she could see Solitaire, stripped, wading into the water. Or was he stripped completely? The obscuring salt cedar branches, the dappled reflections on the water made that impossible to tell. Even naked, the man remained camouflaged somehow.

Annoyed by her adolescent curiosity and reacting with even more adolescent rebellion, Gayle wrenched open the bottle of sunscreen lotion, pouring it on with frustrated, rough sweeps of her hand.

The sun felt warm, even as it ebbed into evening. It angled across her closed eyelids as she lay back, its heat now gentling instead of searing. The dry desert breeze whispered over her anointed skin, wafting away an elemental union of oil and water.

An invisible, variegated incense of sun-simmered desert flowers blanketed Gayle with scent. Her skin held itself expectant, dreading the nearly imperceptible touch of some trespassing insect. Solitaire could send them away, but he couldn't keep them away. Her sun-warm lips curved in a smile; she and a desert insect had a lot in common.

There was no sense listening for anything. Solitaire was too distant for even a muted splash to reach her. Gayle stirred on her downy pallet. She pictured him walking out of the spring toward her, water drops spinning from his body like discarded diamonds. She pictured him wordless as ever, kneeling beside her. His touch would be as gently fugitive as butterflies flocking over her body. He would smell of cinnamon soap and sandalwood. The sun would never set.

Her ears heeded a phantom inner melody, a haunting sound with words tuned to her thoughts.

Des-per-ah-do.

She heard an answer, a soft, rasping answer at the edges of her consciousness. Buzzing, and then stopping. Then buzzing again. It was the intermittence that somehow alarmed her.

Gayle listened, her face frowning despite the serenity of her closed eyes. Buzz, buzz, go away, come again another day. I'm waiting for someone.

Her eyes flared open. She wanted to sit up as abruptly as a corpse in a slasher movie, but didn't dare move. Buzzing. He'd mentioned something about that . . . rattlers! Nearby. Rattle*snake*. Or snakes—who knew?

"Sol-i-taire—" Her first call was a whisper. "Solitaire!" Her voice rose in sound and pitch. The buzzing continued unabated in an odd, arrhythmic pattern that sounded chillingly natural.

"Solitaire!"

At last he came lurching through the salt-cedar boughs, damp as she had imagined, but clothed again, as she had not.

"What?"

"Don't come closer! I hear rattles."

He froze before she had finished speaking, listening. She could almost *hear* him listening. The buzz obliged. Gayle caught her breath. Solitaire crouched beside her, pulling the gun from its fleece-lined case. He cocked his head, listening again. Again, the rasp.

Moving as slowly and smoothly as mud, he unwound into a half-crouch and began circling Gayle in a widening circle. His path took him behind her. She shut her eyes and hoped.

The buzz lectured them both for a good long session, then quieted. Even the wind hushed its intermittent breath. Gayle prayed. Silence held.

Then a faint velvet brush touched her throat. Her eyes squeezed more tightly shut. The sensation migrated, slowly, over her collarbones, its touch so slight that it recalled the butterfly legions from her yearning imagination. Gayle gasped almost inaudibly.

"Solitaire . . ." Gayle whispered so softly that the sound hardly left her mouth.

She shuddered at the stillness.

An arpeggio of revived sensation rippled up the center of her torso toward her face. Her eyes flew open. She glimpsed a yellow satin butterfly settling on her lips. Above her head, Solitaire's face hung like a mahogany sun. He was crouched beside her shoulder.

"I . . . didn't hear you," she said, dry-mouthed.

"I'm good at that. I'm also good at rattler slaying."

The rangy-stemmed flower he held to her lips lifted, then bowed to kiss her again.

"Your 'buzzing,' madame. Paperflower—a desert plant with flowers dry enough to mimic a rattler if the wind is right. It's fooled veteran campers."

She sat up, pushing his hand and the flower away. "That was a rotten trick! I was scared out of my mind!"

A comment of Darcy's echoed in her mind: boys are always mean at first to the girls they like.

His fingertip, paperflower-soft—and-rough, brushed her shoulder. "You shouldn't stay here too long," he said. "You might burn."

Maybe it was the way his last word hung on the dry desert air. Or the startled, burning glance she gave him without thinking.

As if an actor in her own secret scenario, Solitaire reclined beside her, his nearing face steeping hers in its long-sought shadow, his mouth softening as he matched his lips to hers. His weight pressed her so deep into the down sleeping bag that, like a fairytale princess, she counted the desert's numberless rocky peas beneath her back.

The moment was all, everything, she could have imagined, desired, asked or hoped for. Her moment. Her dreamed-of lover. But his eyes, something about his eyes. She searched them. Need shone naked in them, and raw, uncut emerald-green desire. But beyond that, they were empty, his eyes, like holes in his head. Gayle squirmed away from the consummation she so devoutly wished, sick at herself and sorry for him.

A shadow flitted over them, a swift, encompassing shadow that moved in a distant drone their pounding blood had kept from their ears until now. Stricken, they stared up, their bodies parted first by second thoughts, then by fear.

Suddenly, Solitaire rolled himself over Gayle, smothering her—not sexually, but protectively. He twisted his head to stare up at the low-flying plane.

"Bloody voyeur! Nosy parker! Sly traipse-along!" If he hadn't been hiding Gayle beneath his body and shielding arms, he would have been shaking a fist at the sky.

The small single-engine aircraft above ignored his taunts, flirtatiously waggling its wings before droning out of sight over the dusky mountains.

Solitaire relaxed enough to roll off Gayle. "Wild Blue," he explained tersely.

"He couldn't see us—see *me*—from up there?"

"He could until I covered you, the randy old goat."

"But why?"

"Maybe saying hello. Maybe following me."

"But why?"

Solitaire shrugged, looking into her eyes. "Why not?" His face descended over hers again.

"No." Her hand fanned on his chest.

"No? You're saying no?"

"Not . . . now, not here. Not this way. Maybe never, maybe nowhere, maybe no way."

He stared at her, his features curdling into disbelief. He could be cruel when he felt threatened, Gayle recalled, shivering in the flattening sunlight.

Right now, he looked more like a killer than a lover.

Des-per-ah-do . . .

♠ Chapter Eleven ♠

Solitaire rolled onto his back, staring at the paling late afternoon sky. A sheet of wind shivered across Gayle, offering her as little comfort as he did.

She wanted to burrow into the warmth of Solitaire, lying beside her on "his" side of the sleeping bag. Instead, she looked at him. A cord in his neck rippled rhythmically as his control fought for its integrity.

Her fingertips reached to quiet the anomaly of this sole flicker of movement in his body, as if to take his pulse.

"Don't." Icy rage and anguish blended in his voice.

Gayle rose carefully on one elbow to see more of his face than his profile. The eyes ignored her, staring blindly at the sky as if he searched for something unseen in it. Gayle looked up, seeing nothing, no clouds, no planes, no birds.

Des-per-ah-do . . .

Gayle hadn't been able to forget that haunting song since the Crystal Phoenix pianist had played it for them, just before breaking into the theme song of the man beside her—Solitaire.

"Solitaire," Gayle mused aloud, thinking of the last song, the first song and the oddly appropriate words to them both.

"Don't." Tension drew his voice tighter than a garrote. Touching him now would be like taming a high-voltage wire, she guessed. Long-hoarded emotions could surge uncontrollably toward her, and she couldn't survive much more of Solitaire's explosive inner electricity.

167

Gayle's forefinger, light as a paperflower, traced the faint vertical worry line above his eyes. Solitaire didn't even blink.

"I can't let you make love to me," she explained softly. "You're right, you don't know how to, anymore. Maybe you never did. I can't let you . . . overwhelm me again. But *I* can make love to *you*, if you'll let me."

His lips worked, folding and unfolding. Gayle's palm cradled the stubble-roughened line of his jaw. She leaned over to smooth her lips against the narrow moat of satin skin surrounding his ear.

"That's what I always wanted anyway," she whispered. "I never needed you to love *me*, I only wanted to love you, to make love to you. Let me, just this once."

He didn't answer. Gayle's tremulous hand slid to his throat and down smooth, tanned skin to the top button of his shirt.

She had his full attention now.

"What do you want?" he asked suspiciously.

"Don't you like it?"

His lips curled in a smile devoid of mockery, self-control, or bitterness. "You know I do. What do you want?"

She sat back on her heels beside him, tilting her head to see his face from another angle. "The Real Me from Kansas wouldn't ever admit to what I want."

So she showed him.

The setting sun reddened as it neared its nightly impalement on the mountain peaks behind her. It cast an ember-soft glow over them, like a weightless blanket.

Around them the desert dimmed. Paperflower rasped unheeded. Wind could not insinuate itself between them. Time abdicated its throne. Death walked softly and carried a dove.

His embrace suddenly loosened. "Are you done with me?" he asked at last.

"For now," she conceded. "It's getting dark."

He buried his face against her neck. "I haven't even asked if you were protected," he said self-accusingly. "I'm afraid I didn't even care before. I've never known a woman I had to worry about."

"Protected?"

"From consequences."

"Oh, that. Yes . . . and no."

He absorbed the phrase. "You said that once before, about your marriage. I misunderstood. I don't want to again."

"Well, it's the same thing. No, I'm not using contraception and, yes, I can't get pregnant. You don't have to worry. I'm so used to it that I'd forgotten about it."

"Can't get pregnant? Are you . . . unhappy about that?"

She sighed. "I wouldn't know that I couldn't if I . . . we hadn't tried. But it was years ago, when we were first married. And we liked our jobs, and Joe was on such irregular hours, away from home so much. And if I had been able to get pregnant, Joe would only have left more people behind to mourn him."

"You're certain it was you?"

"Certain." Her fingers tightened into his shoulder. "Why? Do you—?"

His laugh was bitter for the first time in days. "I? Why should I harbor thoughts of offspring? I never knew my parents, never knew why they . . . lost me. My uncle was the surly loner sort." His arms enfolded her. "No, Gayle, I have no ambitions for immortality. I wouldn't want to leave you with an awkward legacy, that's all. If I should—"

She returned his embrace fiercely. "You won't. And you

wouldn't. Trust me to know my own strength, Solitaire."

"Strength is the issue, isn't it? I thought my quandary, my life, was too hopeless to ask anyone to share it. Yet you've faced losses that are much more terribly real. Mine are all imagined, mine are only ghosts of what might be . . . mine are unfaced, really."

She answered him with her love, clinging to him so that he had the excuse of something to cling to, kissing him until he became obsessed with kissing her back, until his ghosts were immured behind a wall of all-too-solid flesh. He broke their embrace, finally, a freer man.

Solitaire's smooth palm patted her flank. "You better crawl into the sleeping bag. It's much to cold out here for this sort of thing."

She groaned agreement, slipping into the inner softness to wait for his presence. Instead she heard a rustle and the brusque sealing of a zipper.

"Where are you going?"

"We're hardly ready to camp for the night. I'll get the pack. And the flashlight.

"Be careful," she fretted. "It's not fair, me lying here all warm and safe, and you lugging things in the dark."

"No, it isn't. It's called men's work. Maybe you can make it up to me when I get back."

"I'll do my darnedest," Gayle promised happily.

Gravel scattered at the impress of departing footsteps.

"Solitaire?" The miniature hailing stopped. It was completely dark now. Gayle had never even noticed the sun going down. "I love you," she said quickly, before he could claim he was too far away to hear her properly. The dark was silent and he was still. "Solitaire?" She couldn't help sounding anxious.

"It's all right, Gayle," he answered finally, as if the words had been so distant it took a long time to find them. "I love you too."

The gravel began chattering again, its gossip dying as he moved farther away.

Gayle hugged herself within the sleeping bag's warm confines. The lyrics of a familiar song rolled through her lazy mind, then drifted away.

Solitaire lay in the dark and counted stars.

They were different from the ones he'd known in Australia. For the first time, a spasm of loss for forgotten stars twisted through him.

Beside him, Gayle slept the deep slumber of the sexually sated. He'd rarely stayed with a woman long enough to sleep afterward. Perhaps that was why he had fallen in love with Gayle—he'd quite literally slept with her.

His hand bridged the small gap between them to trace a path alongside her torso. He felt the heat and draw of her, enjoyed knowing that ineluctable pull was still there. She had mentioned death in passing. His body stiffened again. Death was not a thing to mention in passing, at least not to him.

His teeth clamped together, his lips tightening into their customary tension. Now, he supposed, they would find him and kill him, now that he had more than his life to lose. It was just as well he'd had no time or daylight to build a betraying campfire. From now on, he and Gayle must exercise triple caution, get themselves out of the desert and into some sort of safety.

On these troubling thoughts, he let sleep pull him down into the uneasy state of most of his nights. Sleeping, he listened for footsteps.

They came pattering toward him later—much, much later, when a feeble smudge of dawn pinked the eastern sky. Sly, endless steps rattling over the stones.

Solitaire's eyes flew open into a starless sky and falling raindrops. Beside him, Gayle stirred.

"It's nothing, love," he calmed her if not himself. "Just rain."

"On the desert?"

"Even on the desert, sometimes it rains. Everything needs a little water sometime."

She was silent a moment, then snuggled against him. "That's English, isn't it? To call people love?"

"I suppose so."

"Well, I adore it."

He felt hesitant and a bit silly but somehow compelled to say what he felt. "I adore you."

Her hand squeezed up between them to stroke his bearded cheek. "You're going to become a rather schmaltzy fellow, aren't you, Solitaire?"

"Probably," he agreed placidly.

"Indubitably," she corrected. "We've got to learn to speak the same language. And get as schmaltzy as you want. I love it, love."

"Go back to sleep."

She complied by pushing deeper into his arms. Solitaire closed his arms around her and drifted into a deep, early-morning slumber, smiling.

"God must approve, even if we are fornicators," Gayle mused, staring dreamily at the clearing sky.

Solitaire choked on the cold breakfast of dried beef and trail mix he'd supplied them. They were sitting under the shelter of the wide-armed salt cedar tree, snug as crackers in a tin. The rain had stopped, the sandy soil was rapidly drying and the sky overhead was burning bright blue again.

Gayle pointed to the sky. "Look, a rainbow. God must approve."

"Gayle, love—" He hated disillusioning her, maybe because he was beginning to cherish illusions himself. "There's always a rainbow after it rains in the desert."

"Every time?"

He nodded. "Every time. Fact of nature. Mere routine. It doesn't mean a thing, except that it rained."

She considered, chewing thoughtfully. "It means something to me. It's our rainbow. It just is."

He smiled silently, then pulled her against his side. "Maybe God loves optimists."

"I'm sure He does. And pessimists, too." Her finger stroked the roughness of his cheek.

"Then we've got it covered," he said lightly. "But we have to get moving. None of your delicious games, Miss Gayle, until I'm sure we've either lost or beaten our pursuers."

"Them. I'd forgotten." She slumped back on her battered fuchsia-leather boot-heels. "Solitaire, are you sure they're even coming after us? It seems so . . . deserted . . . out here."

"They always have. I've been sure they haven't, before. And they have. Come on, pack up and we'll get going. The Jeep should be dry by now."

Gayle bent to gather any loose ends of their camp and hand them to him. Solitaire paused in packing to watch her.

"Maybe it's my imagination," he noted, "but those jeans look rather fetchingly fitted this morning."

Gayle groaned in dismay. She came toward him until he

reached out to pull her close. "I'm glad you're happy. We washed 'em, remember? Cotton. They shrunk. These things are so close to me they remind me of you."

"Did I ever mention what I had in mind for nice ladies from Kansas who keep saying provocative things like that?"

"No, but I'm always willing to learn."

He kissed the top of her head. "I don't think I could teach you a thing. Let's go."

Once in the Jeep and on the move again, Gayle pulled the binoculars from the pack and studied the empty horizon. She sighed as she lowered them.

"Nothing I can see. Are we going somewhere special? You were studying that old map again before breakfast."

"You were asleep."

"I was pretending. I was watching you."

"Nosy Parker," he said, grinning. His eyes returned to the desert ahead of them. "Perhaps we *are* going somewhere special. There's supposed to be a cache of hundred-year-old Carson City silver dollars out here somewhere. I've a notion that map might point us to it."

"Or our rainbow might." Gayle smiled up at the sky and lifted the binoculars. "It's the real thing, bands of violet and red and green, absolutely gorgeous, Solitaire. Or should I call you Sylvester now?"

"Call me 'Lucky.' "

"I think that's a compliment. Maybe the treasure's at the rainbow's end."

"You'd do better keeping your eyes on the ground, looking for a camel," he answered dryly.

"A camel? Really?"

"Really. A camel-shaped rock formation, actually."

"One hump or two," she asked deadpan.

He slapped her knee. "One."

Gayle obediently aimed the binoculars at the landscape instead of the skyscape. "It'd be easier to see something if this Jeep didn't bounce around so much."

"If it was easy, treasure would be found every day."

"Why are you looking for it?"

"I wasn't. I was simply planning on running again. I thought that old map would help us go where no one could find us, or give us some topographical advantage if we *were* cornered. Then . . . I saw something in Van's office. The map corresponds to that old aerial photograph that was also found in the suite Jersey Joe Jackson lived in for almost forty years, back when it was the Joshua Tree Hotel instead of the Crystal Phoenix."

"Who's Jersey Joe Jackson?"

"A mysterious Las Vegas tycoon gone broke and later dead. And a pal of Wild Blue and his cronies."

"No! Not *our* Wild Blue?"

Solitaire chuckled. "How many Wild Blues do you think there are?"

Gayle shrugged. She was listening more to the easy laughter in his voice than what he said. The man from the Crystal Phoenix Baccarat Cove had vanished. The man beside her could afford to laugh and tease, to be eager and to anticipate something, even if it was only tomorrow.

His face radiated confidence and open joy in her company, stirring in Gayle a deep, placid warmth that reduced the tempestuous longings she'd first felt for him to mere ashes. The world seemed a Technicolor soap bubble that sheltered them within its thin, impervious skin. Everything beyond the bubble's vaguely blurred limits washed away like dust on a windowpane.

"Who gets the treasure if we find it?" she asked, playing the game. It had been a long time since Solitaire had played any game but hide and seek.

"I don't know. Whoever the bloody hell it belongs to."

"Then why find it?"

"For the . . . fun of it."

"Makes sense to me." Gayle put the binoculars to her eyes again, not to look for anything but to conceal suddenly gathering tears. "Hey, that's funny."

"What?"

"There's a rainbow in those foothills ahead."

"Rainbows are heavenly phenomena."

"Not this one."

"Let me see those binoculars." Solitaire stopped the Jeep, then pressed them to his sunglasses. "Where?"

"It looks painted into the rocks, bands of color."

"That's not a rainbow, that's mineral strata, probably iron, copper . . . the yellow's likely sulphur. The shiny stuff's mica."

"Red, green, and yellow. Sounds like a rainbow to me."

"Rainbow in a rock . . . Rainbow Rock!"

Solitaire plopped the heavy binoculars into Gayle's lap without so much as a by-your-leave and pulled the map out of his vest pocket. He spread it over the steering wheel, almost puncturing the brittle paper in his excitement.

"Look!" His forefinger prodded a faded notation. "I couldn't quite read it before—Rainbow Rock! And here, here are three letters, off to one side. L.C.R. Last Camel Rock! This is where Jersey Joe must have stashed the silver dollars over forty-five years ago!"

"Where's the camel?" Gayle's binoculars were scanning the distance. "I don't see it."

The Jeep jerked into gear, plunging toward the faint foothills ahead.

"It could have performed a vanishing act over the years,"

he warned, "lost its head, or hump. If there's any outcropping of rock at one end of Rainbow Rock or the other, we'll find the coins."

Gayle looked overhead. "Our rainbow's fading," she noticed.

"Don't worry. I think we're onto a better one. Hang on!"

The desert bumped past them, the same rocks and scrub smudging by, Gayle thought, like the faces you see over and over when riding a carousel. Her fingers excitedly clenched her jeans. It was so much better running *to* something than away from something.

"People've been looking for this for a long time?" she asked.

"Over forty years if you count the Glory Hole Gang. Since the partial horde was found, the greedy have been taking regular stabs at it."

"But you figured it out."

"Maybe." He glanced at her. "Don't make me right before I've a chance to find out I'm wrong."

"What about . . . them?" She glanced behind.

He glanced, too. "I haven't seen any traces since that campfire. Perhaps I'm wrong about that too. Perhaps everything is coming up cactus flowers."

Gayle leaned into the Jeep's forward hurtle, watching the rocks she had spied under magnification grow to the same proportions before her unaided eyes.

Her rockbound "rainbow" didn't have the perfect arch of the sky-born one, or the intensity of color. It was a rainbow only by a good long stretch of the imagination. But Gayle had plenty of imagination, and now Solitaire did too.

In a few minutes, the Jeep ground to a stop under the rusty rock face. The mineral strata arched fifteen feet above the ground, glittering in the strong midday sunlight.

They stood staring at it, then Solitaire turned to look behind them.

"What?" Gayle asked, worried.

"I thought I heard something."

"Surely we'd have seen anyone coming for miles?"

He walked to the Jeep to pick up the binoculars, aiming them at the sky. "I heard something, perhaps Wild Blue again."

"Well, did you?"

"I don't know. Maybe it's a hawk." The binoculars lowered to the land itself and clung there a long time.

"Solitaire. . . ."

"Hush, love."

She waited, for what seemed like minutes. When he lowered the mask of metal from his face, the binoculars, his features had returned to a semblance of their former self, all optimism pressed out of them.

"My God, what is it?"

"A spume of dust." He took off his hat while he slung the binocular strap around his neck. "Coming right for us. As if they had a map."

Solitaire strode to the back of the Jeep to rip open the rifle box and take out the weapon and shells. He turned to study the crumbling cliff face.

"There, that broken ridge of rocks. It'll give us high ground. We'll haul the packs up in case we're pinned down for a while, and the canteens."

He was thinking aloud, hardly aware of Gayle. She grabbed the daypack when he picked up the heavier backpack and followed him up the shifting shale to the apex of the rocky heap he'd indicated.

He grunted satisfaction as he lowered the pack. "Some cover—not much but some. Get the pistol out, and ammunition. I'll try to move the Jeep where it'll be harder to shoot out the gas tank or tires."

But after he'd slid down the incline, Gayle didn't get the gun. She lay on her stomach on her perch thirty feet above the flat desert floor and strained to see what the binoculars around Solitaire's neck had seen—a lethal plume of advancing dust.

Why couldn't it be a government survey team, or ardent outdoorsmen? Why did Solitaire always have to look on the dark side? Why couldn't it be a mistake?

"It was a mistake," he was saying behind her, his voice as hard as the rocks around them. He slid to his belly beside her, lifting the binoculars to his face.

"A mistake?"

"Bringing you along. Everything!"

"Not . . . us?"

"Yes, 'us,' bloody 'us' too! If I'd been watching, instead of dallying with you—"

"Maybe it isn't them," Gayle offered desperately.

Instead of answering, he pulled her under the shelter of his shoulder and pushed the binoculars to her eyes. "Tell me what you see, Gayle."

"A Jeep. With men in it."

"How many?" He sounded like a sergeant baiting a raw recruit for an answer he already knows.

"Three . . . I think."

"Three. Bloody brilliant deduction on my part!"

"Maybe you can kill them, like you said once."

"Not here! With my back against the wall." He stared bleakly at the oncoming vehicle. "Perhaps I never could have, anywhere. I'd have had to ambush them. Perhaps I have no illusions anymore, about love *or* death."

Gayle said nothing. She reached into the daypack for the

scored wooden butt of the revolver Solitaire had shown her how to point and fire.

"I'm sorry," she said again, almost more frightened of the man beside her than the anonymous men coming to kill him. Kill *them*. Solitaire could hurt her. They could only kill her.

His green eyes blazed at her, awash in anger, frustration and bleak love. "Don't die sorry, Gayle. Believe me, I can't recommend it. I don't care about my coming to this, but you deserved better—always."

His hand clenched in the back of her hair as he pulled her face to his for a hasty, bruising kiss before he lay flat to brace the rifle against his shoulder.

Gayle, breathless with fear and desire, stared at the placid desert with its oncoming dust devil of motion. Even up here she could smell the cactus flowers. And the sky . . . she glanced up.

High above, the last shreds of her rainbow dissolved into mist.

♠ Chapter Twelve ♠

The first bullet gouged a carmine hunk from the rainbow's end behind them, spraying their backs with pebbles.

More gunshots followed. Gayle held her fire as Solitaire had instructed, wondering when he'd use the rifle.

He didn't. Ricocheting rocks hailed around them. Shots reverberated off the stones, thundering into echoes in the sere desert air. The oncoming vehicle ground closer, sounding lawnmower loud.

Solitaire braced his shoulder, aimed, and fired. His body jolted as if hit. Gayle's palms broke into sweat on the pistol grip. She knew he was simply absorbing recoil from the rifle shot, but that's how it would look if a bullet struck him.

He fired again. This time, Gayle's body jerked with his. Seconds later, his hat wafted away as if struck by an arrow instead of a bullet.

Solitaire rolled lower behind the rocks onto his back and grinned at her. "Shot out two of their tires. They must be a bit hot under the sweatband about it."

"If they keep firing, won't they eventually hit us?"

"Not if we stay behind the rocks."

A bullet from an oblique angle whined past Gayle's shoulder. Solitaire hurled himself over her prone body to answer the fire with one carefully placed shot.

Someone cursed. Stones chattered into a rockslide as the gunman slid back to ground level.

Solitaire's rifle barrel nosed some loose ham-size rocks at Gayle's knees. "Pile those into a barrier high enough to hold off side shooters. And don't expose yourself!"

Gayle's nails broke at ragged angles as she wrestled the first rocks into position. The iron-rich stone bled a red powder that painted her palms the color of dried blood. She stacked the rocks crudely, trying not to think. It reminded her of constructing a child-size leaf fort back home in Kansas, but these defenses faced a genuine, very adult threat.

"*Shhh!*" Solitaire called for motionless silence with a gesture sharp as a karate chop.

Gayle let her shoulders relax, and the last red rock slid off the rising pile. The gunfire had stopped. Solitaire's face angled toward the empty cloudless sky.

"I hear that drone again," he diagnosed. "They must too."

An eerie silence settled over the recently noisy patch of desert. Even the rocks seemed to be grinding their teeth as the oncoming buzz swelled to ricochet off their impassive faces.

Then, out of the blue, it came—a small dragonfly of shadow in the vast sky, plunging directly toward them.

"Wild Blue," Solitaire breathed. "I was right. But what's that crazy old coot doing?"

On he came, diving lower as if to sweep the desert floor with the Piper's wings.

"He'll hit us!" Gayle cried, cringing.

Solitaire just grabbed her wrist and watched.

The plane swooped over them, buzzing the gunman's Jeep and drawing an updraft of bullets. The Piper lofted away, seemingly untouched, its wings dipping jauntily from side to side.

Solitaire smiled at the aircraft's shrinking silhouette. "There goes an old fighter ace, I wager. Pray he has the sense to see this is one dogfight he can't win and stay away."

"What could he do, anyway?"

"Draw their fire, waste their bullets. Take a few hits and explode or crash. Stay away, old man," Solitaire beseeched the sky under his breath. "This isn't your *war*, either."

"Maybe he'll get help," Gayle said suddenly, hopefully.

"Maybe." Solitaire flattened himself against the rock again, lifting the rifle.

"Isn't that good?"

"Fine. But by the time he gets anywhere to call for help and the help gets organized to come out here and find us, it'll be all over."

Gayle absorbed his words. Solitaire never had been one to candy-coat reality—his, hers, or theirs. She hefted another rock, then doggedly set it atop her low, uneven wall.

She'd already hollowed out a trunk-size depression in the loose rocks at her knees. Reaching for the next building stone, her ragged fingernails caught on something.

"This looks like cloth—old, dirty cloth!"

"People's trash even finds its way out here," Solitaire said.

Gayle worried at the fabric, irritated by its resistance. It was odd how a minor impediment in the face of major catastrophe could seem so intolerable.

The tough old cloth gave finally. Gayle jolted backwards with a dishcloth-size square of blackened fabric in her fist.

Solitaire glanced at it. "Too dark for a flag of surrender, I'm afraid. And I doubt these blokes take prisoners."

Gayle didn't answer, so he glanced at her again.

She was staring into the rocky depression, an expression of wonder making her face look as if it were illuminated by a glow in the ground.

"This is it," she said dazedly. "Rainbow's end. And here's the treasure."

"The end of the rainbow is oblivion," he answered. "Gayle, pull yourself together."

"I'm not hallucinating, Solitaire. Honest. Look!"

She elevated a small, blackened circle and bit down upon it.

"Gayle! That's filthy!" He pulled it from her mouth and fingers, repelled.

"No, it's just *dirty*. It's been under the dirt for over forty-five years, after all. Look, silver coins, dozens of them. Some are even rainbow-colored."

Solitaire rubbed the blackened coin on his shirt while Gayle began shoveling others from the cache. Some flashed mint-silver, others out-blacked the one he held. And some, as she had said, caught the sunlight and reflected back the shifting rainbow shades found in gasoline slicks—magenta, peacock-blue, bright green, and gold.

"So we've found it." Solitaire tossed the coin he'd been rubbing back on the pile. It rang dully. "Better rebury them so those bastards out there don't get it. Is that how you'd like your 'treasure' to end up?"

"No, but maybe it doesn't have to! Maybe we'll win this time, Solitaire."

His laugh was a brief explosion of weary breath.

"Don't you know the queen of diamonds will beat you if she's able? Money's treacherous, Gayle. It's the last thing I ever wanted. And now that I've been seduced into believing that life might be worth living, I'm sitting on top of a fortune with an impossibly short fuse in it.

"Find me a cache of weapons, Gayle. Unearth an army. Buy time with your coins if you can! This stuff"—he picked up a handful and let the coins trickle musically back onto each other—"is worthless."

Gayle studied the silver dollars. Some lay with the

spread-winged eagle side up, others with the classic profile of Liberty in the guise of a Greek goddess.

Here they sat upon a world of wealth, and their lives weren't worth the powder it would take to kill them.

"Solitaire, maybe there's hope yet."

"Where? Over your rainbow? Hope may still grow in Kansas, but it's on its uppers everywhere else. Perhaps Wild Blue will come back in time to catch them afterwards. Perhaps they won't get away with it and the loot, too. Perhaps you'll survive somehow. Perhaps I can manage to kill one."

He hunched over the rifle, murderous in his despair.

"Look! Something is coming over the rainbow—or where the rainbow used to be." Gayle pointed to the sky.

Solitaire didn't take his eye from the rifle sight. "That's Wild Blue again. I recognize the engine hum. I told you there's nothing he can do for us but risk himself."

"What about the other plane?"

"What other plane?"

"The black spot *behind* Wild Blue."

"Other plane." Solitaire reluctantly laid aside the rifle to pull out the binoculars wedged between his prone chest and the ground.

It took him a few seconds to focus on the tiny dark dot bobbing behind the distant shape of Wild Blue's Piper Cub. Then he started laughing.

"That's not a plane, Gayle, that's a, a—" He rolled onto his side, tears of laughter making dusty tracks down his cheekbones.

"Solitaire?" She stared at him. First he'd thought *she* had snapped. Now she had reason to believe he had.

Solitaire just shook his head helplessly. Gayle studied the sky. Wild Blue's plane was recognizable to the naked eye now, and its trailing dot . . . that dot popped into the foreground suddenly, swooping past Wild Blue and then down toward the desert floor at a dizzying speed and impossible angle.

"It's crashing!" she screamed.

Solitaire sobered, but not much. He rolled onto his stomach to watch. "Not crashing—diving. That's no plane, my Kansas love, it's a bloody helicopter!"

"You mean that's 'help'?"

"Just lie down and watch. You've got a balcony seat."

They hung together over the rock lip, watching a dark waspish form dart down at the men on the ground. Bullets sprayed toward it, but seemed to shatter into nothing in the blinding blur of horizontal blades.

Then gunfire spat from the wheeling dark form. Bullets raked the sand and scrub, scribing a circle around the killers' Jeep.

In moments their guns had dropped to the sand and their hands had raised. Solitaire slowly stood, the rifle at his shoulder, and edged down the incline, covering them while the helicopter sank like a giant eggbeater into the nearby sand.

Four men hurled themselves out, dodging the dust storm raised by the overhead blades. Three were armed, one with a small machine gun.

Gayle watched Solitaire and the newcomers pinch shut on the cowed gunmen like a pair of tweezers. The men from the helicopter quickly separated the men from their fallen weapons and bound their hands behind their backs. Solitaire spoke to them while they worked. The newcomers' gun barrels drooped one by one. Solitaire's was the last to lower, and even then he kept half an eye on the bound men. Two of the newcomers hustled the trio into the waiting helicopter.

Finally Solitaire turned to gesture Gayle down.

She came slowly, newly distrustful of the open and loath to relinquish her revolver. Nobody asked her to. When she neared the rescuers, Solitaire drew her suddenly against his left side, his arm around her shoulders.

He looked up to an unruffled sky, where a Piper Cub wheeled like a hungry hawk, and waved broadly. Gayle waved too. The aircraft soared over them, the wings saluting before it droned off into the empty distance once again.

Gayle eyed the four handsomely grim-faced, dark-haired, light-suited men from the helicopter. "Are these the police?"

One of the men grinned. "Better. I'm Nicky Fontana. I own the Crystal Phoenix. This is my brother Rico." A tall slim man who looked remarkably like Nicky bowed. "And these are a couple of my uncle Mario's best boys, ah, Meatlocker"—Meatlocker was the size of two sides of beef both fighting to split the seams of his tent-size suit—"and Bullseye. Their mamas gave 'em more elegant names, but these pretty much tell it like it is."

"Well!" Gayle was impressed. "Where did you get the helicopter?"

Nicky ran a dusty finger under the impeccable white of his collar. "I, um, borrowed it from the tourist helicopter-ride concession on the Strip." He glanced defensively at Solitaire. "When Jill called from Glory Hole—luckily, they just got a phone line installed—with news that Wild Blue said you folks needed help pronto, I couldn't think of any faster way to get here."

Gayle was still impressed. "The maintenance man said that the Crystal Phoenix didn't like its guests being put out, but this is service above and beyond the call of duty."

"And with a smile," interjected Rico, bestowing another courtly bow on Gayle.

"How did you know it was us?" she wondered.

Before Nicky could answer, Solitaire asked a question.

"How did you know to bring some firepower?"

"Hey, Wild Blue may be plane-crazy, Solitaire, but he isn't blind," Nicky answered. "He saw you were on the run when he met you two in the desert. Then, when he saw the fellas trailing you before you did, he turned tail and called for backup. Then he distracted them until we got here. You owe him a lot."

Solitaire smiled tightly. "Right. Well, maybe we can repay him." Gayle, suddenly exhausted, wrapped her arms around his hips and laid her head against his shoulder. "Listen, mate, can you take Gayle back to the hotel in that whirlybird? She needs a rest."

Nicky beamed, all but rocking smugly on his Gucci heels. "I can do better than that. Meatlocker can drive the Jeep to the highway—it's only twenty miles away—and you two can ride back to the Phoenix in the guest limo. I had it follow us out, figuring you guys might be in bad shape by now."

"But how the hell did you know?" Solitaire exploded. "No one at the hotel knew Gayle, never knew she checked in again. She didn't even sleep there that last night. And your employees must disappear on you now and again. You simply dial the substitute roster and fill in. You couldn't even have missed us."

"We did," Nicky said simply.

Solitaire had no answer to that, but turned to the dusty powder-blue Jeep awaiting them. "About Jill's Jeep—"

"Tell her in town," Nicky advised. "Rico and Bullseye can go topside and get your stuff in case you need it."

"Right," Solitaire agreed, helping Gayle into the Jeep. "There are two packs, and some heavy-type bags of Gayle's near some piled rocks. You know how women drag excess baggage along. I'd be obliged if you'd bring those down too."

"Sure thing." Nicky sprang mountain-goat agile up the incline to pass the message to Rico and Bullseye, who were already rooting around atop the rocks.

There was a moment of inaction. Gayle looked questioningly at Solitaire, who winked at her, and then up at the rocks.

"Holy macaroni spumoni!" came a disbelieving shout. "You know what Gayle's *got* up here, Solitaire?"

"Nothing much," he shouted back. "Just a few broken pieces of a rainbow."

Gayle sat on the molded plastic chair, trying hard to keep her gelatinous spine from sliding off. Her fingers smoothed a rainbow-hued 1889 Carson City silver dollar, one of two Solitaire had abstracted from the hoard before the police had taken it, and him, into their firm protective custody.

"For luck," he had said hours before, handing it to her.

"I thought you didn't believe in luck."

"My belief system is crumbling." He palmed another silver dollar and slipped it into his pants pocket.

Now it was after three in the morning, and Gayle hadn't seen Solitaire or the silver dollars since the police had separated her from them. She had been questioned for two hours and dismissed. Solitaire, the police said, they weren't done with.

So she waited, on a hard chair in a cold institutional hallway, wondering what was happening.

"Heads you win; tails you win."

A presence had slipped onto the seat beside Gayle. She glanced up, startled. Seeing a woman in exotic false-eyelashed stage makeup was even more startling.

Gayle's foggy mind produced a name. "Oh . . . Darcy, isn't it?"

"Darcy McGill Austen. I came as soon as my last show was over." Her long, limber arm squeezed Gayle's slumped shoulders. "We've been so worried about you two, Gayle. Are you all right?"

"I'm fine. But they won't let Solitaire go."

"Give them time." Darcy's lashes flashed up to a man standing beside her. "This is my husband, Steven Austen."

He removed a pipe from his mouth to shake Gayle's hand, his gray eyes twinkling like mica in the sun.

"How do you do, Gayle. Darcy's told me a lot about you."

"She doesn't *know* a lot about me."

Steven smiled wryly. "She knows more about people than they think. Even Solitaire." Gayle's face clouded again. "Don't worry, Gayle. I'm sure it'll come out all right. We'll help. If it hadn't been for Solitaire, Darcy and I wouldn't be together right now."

"If it hadn't have been for me, Solitaire wouldn't be in there right now," Gayle returned self-accusingly, jerking her head to the closed door that she never expected to see open again.

"How goes it?" A tiny woman swept by in a blur of buck-skin fringe and long, feathering dark hair. She plunked down on the other side of Gayle. The Viking-tall blond man with her lowered a blanketed bundle to her blue-jeaned knees.

"You must be Jill," Gayle began with a paralyzing choke in her voice. "About your Jeep—"

"Oh, that old heap," Jill interrupted. "Don't worry. It's still running. Johnny's been wanting me to get some reliable transportation anyway. Maybe I will. A Mercedes."

Gayle looked up to the towering Johnny, who must be Jill's husband, and was startled to find a handsome male face wearing pancake base and eyeliner smiling back at her. Then she remembered. This was Johnny Diamond, the singer.

"You must have come straight from your last show too," she deduced.

Johnny Diamond's long muscular form collapsed on the seat next to Jill. He poked teasingly into the blanket, then lifted his tawny eyes to Gayle.

"Yup. I don't know who would have squalled worse if I hadn't, Samantha Jane or her mother. Solitaire did me a good turn too. If he hadn't withheld some evidence of a . . . haberdashery nature, the mother of my firstborn might be in the slammer right now on a charge of wielding a dangerous weapon."

Jill pushed the Western hat back on her head and glared lovingly at him. "If you don't watch it, you won't get a chance at a second-born." She smiled broadly at Gayle. "I'm a pussycat. Don't you believe a thing he says."

"Any news of Solitaire?" The newcomer's voice came imperiously calm.

Gayle looked up to see a patrician blonde woman. Behind her, Nicky Fontana winked broadly at Gayle.

The woman checked her watch. "Honestly, I checked with Captain Judson an hour ago, and he promised they'd release Solitaire in half an hour." A sleek high heel tapped impatiently, then the woman smiled greetings at everybody and gave Gayle a long, intent look.

"You look exhausted!" She came and crouched before

her, taking Gayle's icy hands in her warm ones.

"I'm Van von Rhine. I manage the Crystal Phoenix. Ever since we realized you were missing from your room, we've been worried white about you. But nobody could confirm your movements since the room on your right was empty and the one on your left is always kept vacant—"

"Oh, but somebody saw me move back in."

"Not in the room on your left, surely?" Van said, an odd look on her serene face.

"Yes, that's the room. Seven-thirteen, I guess. When I checked in, there was a man coming out, a stooped, silver-haired man. He even smiled at me."

"He . . . smiled?"

"Yes. Of course, he must have been gone by the time you came looking for information on me because he was carrying this funny old suitcase—you know, the boxy, stiff kind like you see in old movies? I think he was checking out."

Van von Rhine stared into space for a moment. ". . . checked out. Finally. Because he *knew* you'd find it." Her attention clicked back to the here and now, her expression melting with sympathy. "Gayle, I'm so terribly sorry about what you've been through."

"It's not your fault," Gayle said hastily. "I asked for it."

Van von Rhine suddenly smiled, intensifying the color of her inexcusably blue eyes. "Yes, you did. And I think you got exactly what you asked for." Nicky swept a plastic chair behind Van so she could sit opposite Gayle. "Is that one of the coins?"

"Yes, I—here, you can see it."

Van elevated the rainbow-hued coin to the overhead lights like a jewel.

"Toning," she said authoritatively. "The action of sulphur in both the fabric and paper that wrapped the coins all these years adulterated the natural color. I've consulted several numismatists today."

"Then they're not worth anything?" Darcy asked.

"Au contraire, my dear Darcy," Nicky put in mischievously. "Some collectors would pay even more for a naturally altered coin like this. And most of the coins are pure shining silver. Mint condition."

"The question is," Johnny said suddenly, "who do they really belong to?"

Van's blue eyes flashed impishly. "The courts have been waiting for claimants to appear since the partial hoard was found. It appears there aren't any anymore. The state, of course, will get a portion. It is 'treasure,' after all. Jill and Johnny are entitled to what they found. And the rest"— Van's eyes moved to Gayle—"belongs to Gayle."

"Oh, my." She looked at all the strange faces, suddenly so familiar. Friends, she thought. Family. Solitaire's friends and family. "At least I'll be able to afford a good lawyer for Solitaire—"

Nicky opened his mouth to say something, but another voice intervened.

"Forget the lawyer. They don't want me."

Solitaire Smith stood before the closed door, looking gritty, grimy, and three-quarters dead.

"You're free?" Gayle stood up and, having managed that, could move no more.

He moved toward them in slow motion, as if he'd sat for so long he'd forgotten how to walk.

Johnny stood and scraped his empty chair around so Solitaire could sit between Van and Gayle. But Solitaire braced himself on the chair back and remained standing.

"What keeps you birds from your downy slumbers?" he

wryly asked the gathered Crystal Phoenix crew. "Not the ambition to become jailbirds, surely?"

"We were worried about you." Darcy stretched out a long arm to rest her hand on Solitaire's a moment. "I don't think you've formally met my husband, Steven."

The men shook hands, both diffident for different reasons.

"I'd, ah, like to sit down with you sometime and pick your brain," Steven confided uneasily. "For my books. They're adventure stories, you know. I thought you might be an expert source on . . . various things. I haven't had much adventure myself, outside a classroom."

"Darcy's all the adventure you need!" Nicky hooted.

"And, Solitaire, you know Johnny," Jill put in by way of introduction.

"Not formally either." Solitaire's weary smile broadened. "But I've always liked a good minstrel." A great blond-haired paw batted out to shake a lean brown hand.

"Is there anything we can do for you?" Van inquired in her best looking-after-guests voice.

"Not . . . really." Solitaire slowly moved into the friendly circle they formed and sat in the empty chair next to Gayle. "Perhaps you could introduce me to this young lady—"

Gayle grabbed his hand in both of hers and hung on. "Solitaire, what happened in there? You look as if you'd had the breath knocked out of you."

"I've just had my past . . . rearranged," he admitted, leaning his head against the dirty green wall. The bright overhead fluorescent lights didn't even seem to faze his upturned eyes.

Gayle's touch turned compulsive. "Solitaire, do you know why now?"

He nodded. "And who and for what. It seems I'm not Sylvester Smith, after all, however much you've grown attached to that mellifluous name. The police have been plugging into computers all over the globe all night—Interpol, Scotland Yard, Australia. Now that they got their hands on two of the hired blackguards, they had a hope of tracing them to the one who employed them."

"And—" Everyone leaned forward, spellbound.

Solitaire savored his audience, then let his eyes find Gayle's. He spoke to her alone.

"It seems my 'uncle' was never my uncle, just a caretaker who took me on when my parents died. It seems my name is Sylvester, after a fashion. Reed Warwick Silvestre, and that's why someone wanted to kill me."

"For your name?" Jill was indignant. "That puts a heavy load on parents." She nervously studied Samantha Jane Diamond in her lap.

Solitaire smiled with resignation. "For what went with the name. An English fortune. It seems my father was a rogue first son of a wealthy family. Ran off to Australia during World War Two, married, sired me, got malaria, and died, along with my mother, but not before depositing me in the Dead Centre with a balmy 'uncle' who called me 'Sylvester' out of a warped sense of humor.

"In the meantime, the old folks at home in jolly old England died. The second son's head didn't rest easy under its new title as long as I lived somewhere in the world."

"Title?" Gayle finally dared do what everyone else had been dying to do—interrupt this incredible tale.

Their kind attentive faces turned to her strained white one.

Then Gayle did something she most decidedly didn't want to do. She fainted.

"I'm so embarrassed."

"Don't be," Solitaire consoled. "It was an impeccable finish to a rather melodramatic moment."

"I haven't fainted since Terrible Tommy Swanson put a garter snake down my pinafore in grade school."

"I wager you had breakfast that day, and lunch. You've been out on the desert for several days, Gayle. It'll take a while to feel back to normal."

"Who wouldn't feel back to normal here?" Gayle leaned against the luxuriously padded headboard and studied the huge hotel room. "It was so sweet of Van and Nicky to give us this room, and my clothes are all in it . . . and everything."

"Van doesn't miss a thing. As soon as your room turned up full of your clothes and empty of you, she checked into the stalled elevator incident. When I disappeared, too, she began to put two and two together."

"And now she's done it again," Gayle announced, spreading her arms wide. She was wearing her favorite jumpsuit and no shoes. The fuchsia boots reclined in the nearest wastebasket. "This is a gorgeous room. Showers are okay, but I can't wait to try that Jacuzzi." Gayle eyed the oval sunken bathtub centered between two long, mostly empty closets.

"Wait," Solitaire advised cryptically.

"And champagne on ice . . . and flowers. Van certainly was thoughtful."

"Gayle, love. This all isn't here just for us. She gave us the bridal suite."

"*Oh.*" Gayle's palms covered her warming cheeks. "Maybe we should have asked for separate rooms, for appearance's sake."

"And have them laugh us to kingdom come? Wild Blue's spread the tale, believe me."

Gayle bounced on the bed to see the water-mattress hula like Jell-O. "Let's open the champagne."

"Later. I've an errand to run." Solitaire was at the door.

"Oh?" Gayle sounded vaguely hurt.

"I've got to get some new duds." He glanced at his travel-stained clothes. "*I* didn't have a full suitcase of fresh clothes stashed anywhere. Nicky's given me a hotel credit line. Between the Kreugerands I had salted in my kit for traveling money, my share of the found silver dollars, which are worth hundreds of thousands, and my English inheritance, it appears that I'm a rather worthwhile fellow to cultivate, even in Las Vegas."

"Solitaire, everyone loved you before that."

"I know. It was my outgoing charm and indefatigable sense of fun!"

Gayle hurled a heart-shaped white satin pillow at the crack in the door that was closing on his clean-shaven face. Then she sighed and lay back on the cradling bed. It was all so bizarre. They'd never believe her back in Kansas.

She couldn't wait to tell Connie and Kelly that the man in the Baccarat Cove was really a lost heir, an English lord. And a soon-to-be American millionaire. All accomplished, of course, when the bureaucrats of three continents got their acts together . . . She must have dozed because the next thing she knew, the door was cracking open again and an elegantly shod foot was kicking the fallen pillow aside.

She sat up. "Solitaire?"

"You may well ask." He stepped fully into the room, a tan man in a well-cut pale three-piece suit. "Nicky's favorite men's shop."

"Oh, that Nicky's a sharp dresser all right, but where are your . . . old clothes?"

Solitaire pointed a disdainful thumb downward. "Dumpster."

"Oh, you didn't! You might want a souvenir. I kind of liked those clothes."

"I've got a souvenir." Solitaire ambled over to the bed, seeming a bit shy and looking much too civilized.

He pulled a small box from one of his smart new pockets in his smart new jacket and presented it to her. Gayle opened it cautiously, half afraid of what would be in it— some expensive bauble that would scare her more than please her.

"You shouldn't have. The hotel boutiques are so over-priced and—"

She lifted the piece of jewelry from its velvet nest. It was a ring, a plain thin gold band with a six-pronged mounting in which rested a diamond . . . solitaire. A small, modest-size diamond solitaire, not quite a half-karat, the kind of ring a baccarat referee might be able to afford if he saved his money for months.

The beginnings of a nervous smile played across Solitaire's tension-strung mouth. "Do you . . . approve?"

"Solitaire, it's—perfect!" Gayle slipped it on her ring finger. "But it's so . . . bloody . . . ostentatious for Kansas!"

"Forget Kansas." He sat on the bed and pulled her down with him. "I have this fantasy, you see. It may strike you as a bit kinky, but that's what bridal suites are for, love.

"I see us beside . . . this desert water hole, with nothing but the clothes upon our backs—which will shortly be off our backs—some survival gear, and each other. No champagne, no bouquet of roses, no Jacuzzi fizz, only natural spring water and the smell of the desert roses in bloom.

"I see us listening for the hiss of paperflower instead of the buzz of a telephone. We feel the desert wind instead of the air conditioner. But one thing's the same. We are alone. Completely alone. And I lean to you, and you lean to me, and—"

He did, and she did, and they did.

♠ Chapter Thirteen ♠

The Last of Louie's L'amours

As I have noted before in my memoirs, thirteen is my lucky number, so it is only fitting that I should have the last word at this precise point.

I wish I were able to report that all turns out hunky-dory, but that only happens on the silver screen. As for Mr. Solitaire Smith, aka Mr. Reed Warwick Silvestre, it does indeed transpire that he is the long-lost spawn of the great Norman-English family of Silvestre and worth his weight many times over in pounds sterling.

He and the single-minded little doll from Kansas, Miss Gayle Tyson, do indeed tie the marital knot, with all three of my favorite Crystal Phoenix couples in attendance as well as the Glory Hole Gang, all wearing new dungarees.

The old dudes are feeling their oats, not to mention their bridal champagne, seeing as how Gentleman Johnny Diamond and his wife, Jill, and Mr. Solitaire Smith, now Lord Reed Silvestre, and his wife, Gayle, contribute a sizable portion of their silver dollar loot to the old gents' ghost-town restoration project.

This festive occasion does not take place at some tony church but at the Lover's-Knot Wedding Chapel down on the Strip, just up the boulevard from the Araby Motel, with which establishment the bridal couple seems to have some bizarre sentimental attachment.

Me, no one invites to the wedding. I do not berate my fate overmuch on this score, as weddings strike me as more than somewhat sentimental affairs, not to mention dangerous.

After the bridal couple return from a honeymoon to, of all places, Australia, they divide their residence between some high-falutin place in England and Las Vegas to lead a life of leisure, of which it only behooves me to approve, given my own lifelong predilections.

It seems the bridegroom tires of the globe-trotting existence, not to mention earning his daily bread, and the bride can think of no good reason to spend time managing a bank when she could be managing their personal funds and finding it a much more challenging job.

Myself, all this fiscal and emotional bliss strikes me as somewhat redundant. It is possible my outlook is affected by an event of an earth-shaking nature which occurs while Mr. and Mrs. Reed Silvestre, whom she still calls 'Solitaire' in private and not-so-private moments, are on safari or whatever one is on in Australia.

This event is nothing less than the departure of the Divine Yvette from my purview. I am first aware of this catastrophe, and I do mean cat-as-tro-phe, when I spy the Divine Yvette ambling through the lobby on her twenty-four-karat neckpiece.

I am horrified to hear her companion, the film star, Miss Savannah Ashleigh, check out, cooing in a loud voice what a splendid time she had at the Crystal Phoenix and how she will recommend it to all her very best friends. Naturally the assistant manager goes white as a fishbone, but she manages to choke out a gracious answer in the best Crystal Phoenix tradition.

I arrange to stalk near the Divine Yvette, who winks at me and sways elegantly from side to side against Miss Savannah Ashleigh's silken hose. I am man-about-town enough to know that the Divine Yvette is indicating a preference for swooning against my manly chest.

Alas, it is not to be. Miss Savannah Ashleigh bends down, and in the presence of the entire lobby, picks up—picks up!—the Divine Yvette and carries her from my life. The Divine Yvette gives one heart-rending, slightly miffed cry. I tail them to the entrance, where a long black limo is purring at the curb.

The last I see of the Divine Yvette is her sorrowful lettuce-green eyes watching me through the deep window tint on the limo as it pulls into the hot Las Vegas morning sun.

Needless to say, I am most distraught at this cruel twist of fate. I wander, hardly knowing where my stumbling feet lead me, to the rear of the hotel and sink into the shade by Chef Sing Song's most excellent carp pond.

I am so despondent that not even the tail flick of an Acapulco Gold—a most tender, tasty variety of goldfish—can tempt me. It is then that I see Nostradamus, my old friend, the bookie, upon whom I have not laid eye or whisker in some time.

"Ah, Louie," says he, "even the wise grow old.

"Eat, drink, and be merry before you grow cold."

Then he bends down and flips this plump, juicy carp of an aristocratic breed onto the flagstones, where it flaps most becomingly.

Well, you know me. I am never one to turn down an old friend on the offer of a free lunch.

Tailpiece:

Midnight Louie's Last Word

At last! The treasure is out in the open. How come I did not get any of the loot, though?

You didn't find it.

That is another gripe. Once again I was cut out of the action. I may be a fine and dandy narrator, but I want to get in there tooth and nail.

Sharper than a serpent's tooth is the bite of an ungrateful collaborator, particularly if he is feline. You are lucky I've been able to restore your cut chapters in these reissued editions. Even your modest presence was a problem to the Quartet's first editor.

Good! I like to cause problems for villains, even if they are offstage.

You are a true crime-fighter, Louie. It is amazing the hoops that romance writers were put through years ago, often for no reason. One romance writer had the Chevy Blazer in her romance changed to a Ford Bronco. This was long before every major corporation seemed to own a piece of every other one, so it wasn't as if Ford was the house brand. I'll never know why, in this book, Gayle's hometown of Canton, Kansas, was changed to Canton, Ohio, other than the fact that Canton, Ohio is well know. But many town names repeat themselves all over the map. Besides, I used a running theme playing on Gayle's name and Wizard of Oz imagery. Those metaphors and figures of speech were stripped out, or made meaningless by making "Kansas" into

"Ohio." The scene where Gayle chases Solitaire's Jeep through the desert scrub is a parallel to Dorothy Gale running through the poppy field before reaching Oz, for instance. I'll never know if the first editor didn't like my use of the classic tale (and I use literary references in all my fiction) or simply didn't get it and thought the ignorant author meant the Canton in Ohio. This was the kind of wholesale change that was too late to fix by the time I realized the books had been cut without my permission.

While editing these reissued Quartet books, I discovered the impossibility of restoring published books to their original form. I thought my 15-year-old computer diskettes were complete, but I found only post-revision versions and post-cutting manuscripts. We authors like to think books are written in concrete form, but they become very fluid through the editing process, and even more so if we neglect to back them up in many forms. And, of course, we never have enough time to do an absolutely definitive job of it.

Going back in time is quite a trip. While working on these books I was struck by how well a Damon Runyon tone fits contemporary romance: the larger-than-life setting and sentimental characters make a good contrast to the slightly seamy background of an entertainment Mecca like Broadway or Las Vegas. Of course your narrative voice is the most Runyonesque element in the Quartet and your mystery series.

I also forgot some elements in the Quartet that later showed up in the current series: mention of the Lovers' Knot Wedding Chapel, now run by Electra Lark, and even that the Divine Yvette and her mistress Savannah Ashleigh were introduced in this last book.

I am shocked to my claw-sheaths! How could even a human forget the Divine Yvette? Frankly, were it not for

her presence on the scene, this book would have little sex appeal for my many readers.

I must say that your infatuation with the Divine Miss Y made a nice parallel to Gayle's obsession with Solitaire.

That Solitaire is my kind of guy, a macho mean-street prowler of the first order. Why did he have to go all mushy on me?

This is a romance series, Louie, not a mystery one. Besides, in this book, I wanted to explore the nature of infatuation. Usually in romances, the couple gradually get together. I wanted to look at a relationship where they got together too fast and then had to rebuild. Also, the theme of Beauty and the Beast is a classic one. The whole romance genre is about female love transmuting male lust into a committed relationship. So romance readers really like to see an overly macho guy reveal his sensitive side.

Gag me with a sagebrush hairball! Fast, slow, it is all the same to me as long you promise to bring the Divine Yvette back to town frequently and often. As for showing anyone my sensitive side, I guess that would be the underside of my sandpaper tongue, and I keep that well to myself. Sensitive side, indeed. Are you trying to get me killed here, or what?

Actually, an endangered protagonist certainly increases the narrative tension, which is why you've frequently risked life, limb, and limber tail in your later cases.

And I hope to continue doing so for many, many cases, and novels, to come. What am I saying? I am putting my own neck on the line here.

Being a feline P.I. is a dirty job, Louie, but somebody has to do it. I'm just glad that you are not an average cat in any respect, including being limited to the usual nine lives.

I guess that first editor of mine found *that* out!

Thanks to your readers. Say goodnight, Louie.

Goodnight, Louie fans. See you in my next hot cases in cold type.

4/01